SPECIAL MESSAGE TO READERS

THE ULVERSCROFT FOUNDATION
(registered UK charity number 264873)
was established in 1972 to provide funds for research, diagnosis and treatment of eye diseases. Examples of major projects funded by the Ulverscroft Foundation are:

- The Children's Eye Unit at Moorfields Eye Hospital, London
- The Ulverscroft Children's Eye Unit at Great Ormond Street Hospital for Sick Children
- Funding research into eye diseases and treatment at the Department of Ophthalmology, University of Leicester
- The Ulverscroft Vision Research Group, Institute of Child Health
- Twin operating theatres at the Western Ophthalmic Hospital, London
- The Chair of Ophthalmology at the Royal Australian College of Ophthalmologists

You can help further the work of the Foundation by making a donation or leaving a legacy. Every contribution is gratefully received. If you would like to help support the Foundation or require further information, please contact:

THE ULVERSCROFT FOUNDATION
The Green, Bradgate Road, Anstey
Leicester LE7 7FU, England
Tel: (0116) 236 4325
website: www.ulverscroft-foundation.org.uk

IN SICKNESS AND IN HEALTH

Motherless, with a cold and distant father, Sophia Baxter-Lodge sought comfort with Isaac, the stable lad. But when Sir Kenneth found them locked in an embrace, he drove them both out in a fury. Isaac was sent to fight in the Peninsular War, and Sophia shipped off to a ladies' college. Now she is back home, and Sir Kenneth is determined to marry her off to the charismatic trader Mr Lucas Huntley. But Sophia's heart still lies elsewhere . . .

VALERIE HOLMES

IN SICKNESS AND IN HEALTH

Complete and Unabridged

LINFORD
Leicester

First published in Great Britain in 2020

First Linford Edition
published 2022

A catalogue record for this book is available from the British Library.

ISBN 978–1–4448–4983–7

Published by
Ulverscroft Limited
Anstey, Leicestershire

Printed and bound in Great Britain by
TJ Books Ltd., Padstow, Cornwall

This book is printed on acid-free paper

Prologue

Winter 1799

Sophia Baxter-Lodge tried to run into her mother's bedchamber, to break through the barrier of her father, the doctor and Brent.

'Stop her, Brent!' Sir Kenneth Baxter-Lodge ordered his manservant.

Sophia was physically restrained, preventing her from being at her mother's bedside while she was giving birth. Her mother was crying out and she needed Sophia. Sophia wanted to tell her not to worry and that all would be well. At that precise moment, while the doctor and her father were holding her back, she hated all men.

Her father's angry eyes glared at her. 'Show some dignity!' he snapped and pointed an accusing finger only inches from her face. Sophia felt like biting it — hurting him so badly that he too would scream out. His words were as damning to her ears as her mother's cries.

'Let me know when it is all over,' he told Brent. Looking at Sophia briefly he shook his head and walked away. 'I shall wait in my study.'

When Dr Aimes re-entered her bedchamber after tending to her mother, Sophia struggled to try and see through the doorway, but Brent's grip was far too tight and he shut the door behind him.

Sophia lashed out with her heel, wriggling free from Brent's chubby hands as he gasped in pain. With one more swift back kick to his shins, she managed to break away. Ignoring his irate calls, she ran straight for the servants' passage, flinging wide the hidden door. Sophia didn't want to be alone, not tonight — not ever! She needed to be with her friend Isaac.

Shadows surrounded Sophia as she ran down the dimly lit passage, cutting between the kitchens and the laundry. The servants' quarters were a place where her mother forbade her to go — ever.

But tonight it was as far away as she could get from her mother's anguished screams — the chilling sounds that tore at Sophia's heart.

The uncarpeted stone of the servants' steps was surprisingly cold and hard to her silk-slippered feet. This sparse stairwell led to an empty stone-flagged corridor bereft of any furnishings. It set it apart from the rest of her home, Fenton Hall, where for the past ten years she had been raised in warmth and comfort. Yet these arteries were the vessels that kept everything functioning with servants seeing to their daily chores, out of sight and mind, but essential for the family's life to continue as it always had done, smoothly and undisturbed. Her father spent most of his time in the city so really it was her and her mother's home. Yet tonight nothing was as it should be.

Hearing a movement ahead of her, she ducked behind a pile of laundry discarded within a corner of a large stone storage room and hid.

Sophia shivered; her nightdress provided little warmth. Isaac should not see her like this, but where else was she to go? She must somehow cross the cobbled yard to the stables. Two maids ran past carrying more water and towels. She watched the steam rise from the jugs as they went by.

Another maid returned and heaped soiled linen on top of the pile of laundry. Sophia reached up to gain a hand hold, realising she had to escape quickly. When her fingers touched something wet, she stilled. Blood! Mother's blood! Surely not? Sophia's own ran as cold as the stone around her as a gasp escaped her trembling lips. She could not run away anymore. Time had frozen and trapped her inside its icy shell.

'Grab her!' Brent's voice echoed.

Sophia's head shot up. She took a few steps back but stopped with a bump as she pressed against the damp wall.

Mrs Gribbins, the cook, moved forward. Sophia saw the concerned figure of Isaac who was watching from behind Brent. Robert Judd, although a head shorter than Isaac, placed a hand firmly on his friend's arm preventing him from stepping forward. The two young men stared at her together; she saw the pain in Isaac's eyes and could not fathom what was in Judd's, but there was nothing either could do to help her. Sophia knew it and, even in her distress, shook her head. Isaac nodded at her. He understood he must not interfere.

Brent tried to grab her. Sophia fought back like a wild animal. Before she could escape again, Mrs Gribbins threw a clean sheet over her so that she was confined. Brent picked her up and swung her over his shoulder to be taken unceremoniously back upstairs.

Jostled along, she realised that all other sounds had abated. No more screams. No more tears. Nothing! Silence ensued. An eerie silence as if . . . as if . . . Sophia's body slumped, for she too had given up the fight for the night. She would wait for first light. Her mama must be resting.

Tomorrow everything would return to normal.

Little did Sophia know that nothing would ever be the same again.

1

Summer 1809

'Sophia!'

'Yes, sir?' Sophia greeted her father in a polite, detached manner. Their relationship had remained strained ever since her mother's death ten years ago.

'I need you to make arrangements for a dinner party for my dear Cynthia on the 19th. It will be held in the garden if the weather is pleasing, or if not, in the orangery. See that there is adequate provision for ten people and make room for a quartet to play for an hour. I expect it to begin at 3pm. Guest rooms need to be made available for the ladies to freshen up. The party will then continue with dinner and evening entertainment: charades, games — have the billiard room made ready for the gentlemen and there will be more music of course.

'I want you to sing two songs before

dinner as the guests gather, something inspiring and patriotic, and then you may dine with us. You will show the ladies to the withdrawing room and then make sure that the servants clear all away and leave everything freshly laid for morning. The men will break their fast early as a shoot has been arranged and the ladies will arise by the time we have returned.'

Sir Kenneth Baxter-Lodge stopped to cough and take a breath before continuing. 'Arrange for a buffet lunch to be set in the oak dining room and please be there as each guest departs. I want everyone to be gone at least two hours before our dinner is served, which will be set for me, Cynthia, you and our guest Mr Charles Huntley.'

Sophia's father's marriage to Cynthia had brought him money in abundance, and Cynthia had the youth and energy to keep his friends and business associates entertained. Since her arrival, the fortunes of his estate at Fenton Hall had vastly improved; it was lively with dances, gatherings, hunts and assemblies.

The woman was only five summers older than Sophia. Sophia found Cynthia flighty, but there was no malice between them. This change in the family's fortune also made Sophia an heiress of some note.

Sir Kenneth turned away from her and Sophia knew she was being dismissed. However, she was not going to be so easily turned away.

'Who is Mr Charles Huntley?' she asked.

'Mr Huntley is an associate of mine and a dear friend of Cynthia's family. I would ask you to make a particular effort with your appearance — ask Cynthia for guidance. You will wear something becoming. I need you to be pleasing to his eyes.' Her father's attention was instantly returned to the papers in front of him. Laying the letter he had been holding down on his desk he flipped the tails of his jacket before sitting ready to pen his reply.

'I always aim to be 'pleasing', Father.' Sophia watched his head slowly lift, his worldly eyes looking straight into her own challenging ones.

'I am sure you do try, but you will wear the dress that Cynthia has chosen for you and make sure that you have your hair made up. It is not an unbecoming shade of brown — walnut, I suppose, but she will see that it is decorated and tinkered with to lift its weight away from your face. Your features may be strong rather than feminine, but she will try to make them as appealing as she can. Now, I have work to do and you have your instructions.' Sir Kenneth waved his hand in the air to dismiss her.

Sophia's eyebrows rose. Did he really need to make her feel so unattractive? What was wrong with being strong? She did not move but stared at the top of her father's balding head. 'Why is it so important that I, your daughter, who serves to keep house for you, should appear so appealing for this man in particular?' she persisted and saw that a deeper shade of red had appeared on his stubbled cheeks.

Sir Kenneth slowly raised his face. 'You resent being in charge of the household, do you? Perhaps you would like me to employ a housekeeper to organise things around the Hall for you! I could easily find someone who would take control. Cynthia is not able like you are, to cope with managing such affairs —'

'Nor am I, Father!' Sophia stared back at him. 'I only know what I have learned from my mother's memory, from the ladies' college where you sent me —'

'You are far more practical than Cynthia, and not so easily controlled by the will of other people. Have you never considered how fortunate you were not to have been thrown into a convent or onto the streets, girl, after consorting with that stable lad? You are lucky to be here at all.'

'Father, I —' Sophia tried once more to explain, despite knowing he would never listen to her. It was all she could do not to scream at him — *I am innocent!* What good would it do though? She had behaved shamefully and he had seen it for himself. She owed her father, for he saved her from what could have been a ruin of her own making.

Her secret friend had provided much excitement and fun throughout a bleak winter. She had been so happy. Isaac had comforted her when she needed someone to hold her and she still remembered the overwhelming feelings of warmth that had welled through her body as they embraced — they had been young and happy and, foolishly she thought, in love.

But once seen alone in Isaac's presence was once too many. Sir Kenneth had every right to disown her and cast her off, but he had not. He loved her and Sophia was still his heiress.

'Do not dare to try to placate me on this matter — it did not work five years ago and neither will it now. The memory of my daughter, the sole heiress to this grand estate, canoodling with a hired hand will haunt me to my dying day.'

'Father, I never did anything more than —'

'Enough! You have the household

accounts at your fingertips. You write your notes to the suppliers and change them if they do not meet your standards. You have my ear and you have my trust to do these tasks. How many men would trust a daughter in this way?'

Sophia could not prevent her head from jerking back slightly; his message felt like a slap on her cheek. 'Isaac only helped to teach me how to ride, sir.' She swallowed. 'You know this; you left me with Isaac and his father for lessons.' She was holding her hands together in front of her trying hard to keep an even, calm composure. She dearly did not wish to row over this point again. Once this moment had passed it would be buried for both of them forever.

'Every word you utter digs you in deeper. He was a servant boy. You should not even have acknowledged the existence of him, and yet you were wrapped up in his arms.' Sir Kenneth shook his head.

'It was a simple gesture made out of friendship, Father. He saved me from a fall when I was out riding. He stopped me being injured, and . . . and . . . besides, servants are people too!' Her last words were snapped out in a sharper manner than she had intended.

'Now you talk like a revolutionary!' Sir Kenneth balled his fists. 'Girl, I saved you from a much more shameful and desperate fall, if only you would acknowledge that fact.' He shook his head. 'If I had not returned early what else would you have done?'

Sophia's hands balled. This was too much. 'I will ignore that question as it does not deserve an answer, Father! He was my riding instructor and I was grateful for his bravery.'

Sir Kenneth sighed. 'Do not even bother trying to explain yourself. Isaac Dalesman, a common stable hand, is now serving with his beloved horses in the cavalry. Be grateful to me that I bothered to get him a position in the light dragoons due to his father's long service on the estate before him. If he survives he had better not show his face here again. Isaac Dalesman's real penance has been to miss the demise of his own father! Think on that.'

Sophia bit her lip and looked out of the window for the thought cut her heart deeply. Poor Isaac!

'And for that I am deeply sorry, for Joshua was a good man and deserved better of his only son.' Sir Kenneth shook his head. 'Now, you have your instructions and my stated faith in your ability to carry them out. Please do as I have requested without further question.'

Sophia tried desperately to blank out the pain his words regarding Isaac caused her. She had received word from a friend of his, now a lieutenant, that he was alive and well and longed to return for her once the war was won. The letter had arrived in the spring and so she still waited in hope. He would come back to her, with rank, and then they would be together.

'You must befriend Mr Huntley and discover what interests him and report what you find out back to me. Let him walk with you around the orangery, or in the walled garden if the evening is pleasant. Do not go beyond our sight,' Sir Kenneth said, and waved a warning finger at her.

'Why, Father?' Sophia asked quietly.

'Because I ask it of you and you are my devoted daughter, are you not?' He smiled; no answer was needed. 'Now go and do as I say. I have heard his son's engagement was called off, but I do not know why. His son, Mr Lucas Huntley, is nearly thirty, never married and owns land in the colonies and also in London. Why then has he no wife? If it is possible, I would consider a match, depending on what we find out about the man.'

'You would send me off to the colonies?' Sophia was appalled at the suggestion.

Sir Kenneth laughed. 'Believe me, girl, I have been tempted by the thought on many an occasion. No, your cousin Annabelle needs a suitable spouse and her mother and father have asked me to help out. They also want her to move away — far away — as her temper has not improved since childhood, but she is a beauty.'

Sophia was momentarily insulted by the dismissal of the idea that she should not be considered. 'Why do you not just ask his father when you see him?' she asked.

'Because I want to find out what the son's weaknesses are and I believe he will defend his son, but you may very well be able to ascertain something in innocent conversation. Find out if his son is worthy. Now go, or you will have nothing ready for the celebrations and Cynthia will have a fit of the nerves.'

Sophia left him, relieved to have ended their conversation relatively amicably. She felt strangely excited at the prospect of meeting Mr Charles Huntley and setting about on her quest. She was vexed at her father for being so dismissive of her and yet perhaps it was a sign that deep down he may have finally forgiven her the shame of her youthful indiscretion.

2

Sophia's arrangements worked to perfection as usual. The first day went just as she had planned it would, and as her father had instructed, though Mr Charles Huntley had not yet arrived. The guests all seemed satisfactorily entertained and more importantly, Sir Kenneth was happy that the party was being managed well.

'Sophia!' Cynthia was running along the corridor towards her. She looked, Sophia thought, like a wood nymph, one that was slightly worse for wine perhaps. Her youthfulness still shone through those bright eyes, emphasised by her rosy cheeks and happy smile. Sophia could not help but like her even though it made her feel disloyal to her mother's memory, but Cynthia had brought life back to the Hall and, Sophia reluctantly admitted, to her father.

'Is something wrong, Cynthia?' Sophia

asked, knowing if there was she was sure that she would be able to correct it in minutes.

'No, all is excellent!' Cynthia stopped abruptly before her and kissed Sophia on the cheek. 'Thank you for all you have done. I would be lost without you, my dear,' she admitted and was about to run back to her guests when Sophia stopped her, gently holding onto her wrist.

'Cynthia!' Sophia said in an inspired moment. The woman looked back at her; head tilted like a curious puppy on one side. 'Who is Mr Charles Huntley? What is he like?'

'Mr Huntley is an old friend of my father's. He has invested in land in the colonies and your father has lots of good sheep he would like to sell to him. If old man Huntley is willing, your father's stock will help start a new and hardy breed out there. Wherever 'there' is,' she giggled. 'I am married and can only, and rightfully, tend to your father's needs, but you can charm Mr Huntley for your father. Hang on his every utterance, intrigued and beguiled, laugh delicately at his quips and make sure that his plate, glass and goodwill overflow completely. Besides, he has only one eligible son who stands to inherit his father's entire wealth!' Cynthia winked at Sophia. 'Think on that as you dazzle the father, for new or old, money is still money, my dear.' Cynthia gave Sophia a quick pat on her shoulder. 'You should relax these more; sometimes you look so stiff. A young woman's poise should be full of grace.' Cynthia shook her head. 'You will learn,' she said confidently and then drifted back to her guests.

Sophia sighed. She would rather organise a banquet for a hundred people than fawn over an old man like Mr Huntley. She did not doubt that he liked the attention of younger women, but what if he decided that she would make a good companion for his dotage? She hoped beyond hope that he was married to a Mrs Charles Huntley whom he still passionately adored.

3

Mr Lucas Huntley began to curse with a vengeance. Just as he was a mile off the old market town of Gorebeck his horse began to limp. He had been sent to this godforsaken part of the country when he could have been on his way to oversee the preparations for their move to the colonies, as he had to stand in for his father with one of his old cronies, and look over the man's daughter in consideration as a possible wife!

Lucas shook his head. As if he would be interested in a glorified farmer's daughter from the back of beyond. Mind, where he was going, he mused, it would be better if she was a hardy woman and not a delicate creature like his lovely Mary.

'Oh my dear Mary!' he muttered and sighed. So beautiful, so lively, but she would never survive the ocean crossing, let alone the exacting climate they could expect in Australia. He screwed up his face as he buried the pain deep; he needed heirs. He needed sons to help him run the family business and daughters to look after him in his dotage. If he could only stay in Surrey with Mary, but that was not to be, and so here he was plodding onwards to see the farmer's brat!

Lucas's horse neighed wildly nearly throwing him to the ground as it stumbled.

'Damnation!' Lucas snapped as he fought to regain control. Now even the horse had seemingly given up on the idea of his current missive. He took his foot out of the stirrup and slipped his leg over the saddle, jumping to the ground in one smooth move as the horse steadied. He held the reins and waited for it to calm before looking to see what had caused it to react so. His annoyance soon turned to concern when he saw that there was a cut on its fetlock that looked quite deep. He patted the horse's neck — it was hardly the beast's fault — and he decided that he would walk the last mile to Gorebeck town where he could have it tended to. He would need a room for the night as his journey had taken longer than he had hoped and if needs be he would rent another horse in the morning to ride to Fenton Hall.

Lucas made his way down from the moor road to the market in Gorebeck. The church steeple and old dry stone bridge over the river seemed to mark the central point of this community rather than the market square at one end. A coach pulled up in front of an inn as he crested the bridge. He watched a passenger alight and stumble heavily as he stepped out.

* * *

Lieutenant Isaac Dalesman grimaced as he climbed down from the coach, placing his weight unevenly on his one good leg. He tried to hide his unsteady gait as he straightened his injured leg carefully. It was a blessing that he had made it back to Gorebeck in one piece — well almost.

'Your bag, man,' the driver shouted down to him as he untied it from atop the coach. 'Ask the lad over there to give you a hand with it.' The driver dropped the leather holdall from the full height of the coach.

Fortunately there was nothing wrong with Isaac's arms and he caught it before it could hit the ground. The driver's words had shown compassion, but his actions lacked subtlety. Isaac was used to that. He was a soldier of rank; hard won, and he prided himself upon it. Isaac nodded back at the driver.

Isaac wrapped his greatcoat around his uniform and picked his bag up in one hand as he manoeuvred his leg around it with the aid of a cane walking stick in the other. This was not how he had wanted to return to Sophia. At least his condition was only a temporary setback. He limped purposefully towards the inn.

A young lad was leaning against the inn's wall, sucking on a clay pipe as if he was much older than his young years. Isaac wanted to tell him not to grow up too soon, because he would be snapped up to fight in a war on foreign soil where the chances of him actually reaching his maturity would be instantly reduced. Taking the King's shilling made young men, no more than boys, feel brave until they saw the reality of a blood and guts spilling war; not the heroic fate that young minds imagined. It was a waste of life.

Isaac had been fortunate to have been raised up from the ranks, which had protected him somewhat. He had met a captain who had shielded him from the harrowing abuse of those who would have seen him cast back down to the lower ranks where they believed he belonged.

The lad jumped to Isaac's aid and took hold of his bag. 'I can get that, sir,' he said proudly as he picked up the burden for Isaac.

Isaac accepted the lad's offer, but his attention was taken by a stranger walking towards the inn, looking slightly worse for wear and leading a limping horse. 'No doubt you can, but I think that man may need your help more than I.' Isaac pointed with his cane. The tired looking figure was making slow progress with the animal lagging behind.

'Right oh, sir,' the lad said, after placing the bag down just inside the inn's doorway and collecting a coin from Isaac.

Isaac entered the inn, resting on a settle just inside the door for a moment as he readjusted the strapping on his calf. How often he had wanted to do that on the tediously painful journey up country from Hull. Each jolt of the carriage had taken its toll on him as he'd squinted through the pains that had shot up his leg, but he had tried to remain impassive so as not to create undue concern from the lady who accompanied her husband within the cramped space.

When he was ready to stand again and approach the innkeeper he discovered he was not alone. The lad had hastened the stranger's arrival by taking the horse, and both stood before the innkeeper's counter.

'Can I help you, gents?' the man asked.

Isaac and the man answered in unison, 'A room, please.' They exchanged awkward smiles at each other as they acknowledged the other's presence.

'Very good,' the innkeeper said. 'That will be 1s 4d for sharing. Blankets included, food not.' The man reached down under the counter for a key.

Both men blurted out that they had meant to have separate rooms.

'Sorry, but rooms are all taken except for the last one overlooking the street. It's me best one; hence the cost.' The innkeeper shrugged his shoulders, glancing from one to the other. 'There's an auction tomorrow, see, and rooms are all gone excepting the last one.'

'Is there another inn within the town?' the man next to Isaac snapped.

'Yes, but, although I say it meself, ours is the best one, though you may find more female companionship down at the Rabbit and Hare. It is an old style inn, gents, whereas we take in more gentrified people.'

'I would like the room here,' Isaac said, as he looked at the stranger.

'That will be 2 shillings for one, though you can share if you are willing.'

'My horse is stabled here,' the man next to Isaac said. 'Let me share the room for one night and I'll move on in the morning.'

Isaac nodded at the stranger. It was far from ideal, but after spending years with his men in a unit, he was used to the company.

The satisfied innkeeper led the two men up the narrow stairwell to their room.

There was an awkward silence as the two men were left together in the room. They stared at the bed.

'Lucas Huntley,' the man said, holding out his hand.

'Isaac Dalesford,' Isaac replied, shaking Lucas's hand.

Lucas lifted the corner of the blankets.

'Well, I've stayed in worse,' he said, as he dropped them back down. 'Normally, when I was too drunk to realise until I awoke the next day.' He smiled at Isaac, who laughed.

'At least there are blankets,' Isaac added.

'Yes, one each, small mercies,' Lucas replied.

Isaac turned around and sat down on the window seat, grateful to rest his leg. He saw the man stare at his uniform as his greatcoat fell open.

'You are recently returned?' Lucas asked.

Isaac nodded. 'Yes. Lieutenant Dalesman of the 29th.'

'A cavalry man?'

'Was.' Isaac tapped his leg gently.

'Shot in action?' Lucas asked.

'Cut and bruised in the fall when they took down my horse.' Isaac shrugged. 'I was fortunate not to be run through. My horse was not so lucky. Such a shame, he was a fine beast.'

'Your father will be most relieved it

was the beast that fell in action and not you.'

'No, he won't,' Isaac said.

'Bad feelings between you?' Lucas asked. 'I frequently am at cross purposes with my own father. He never listens to me, and yet constantly demands my obedience.'

'No, not that, sir. We were very close. He died a few years ago. I was away and I found out when the letter made its convoluted way to me, but he had long since been placed in the ground. It still hurts to think I missed my own father's funeral. I should have been there for him.' Isaac blinked and then straightened his shoulders, surprised that he had revealed so much.

'My apologies, I presumed it was he who bought your commission,' Lucas said.

'No one bought it for me, I earned it,' Isaac replied, and tried to take the bitter edge out of his voice. He had saved a supplies wagon that his unit was depending on from an ambush, risking his own life to give the warning. He looked down at his leg. He had had dreams of climbing much higher in the army's rankings, even if realistically his origins would no doubt have prevented that from ever happening.

'My apologies again,' Lucas said and smiled pleasantly. 'I have never shared a bed with a real life hero before.'

Isaac was not sure if he was being genuine or sarcastic. The man had a certain charm about him that no doubt would sit well with the ladies. 'I'm no hero. Right place, right time, simple as that.'

Isaac hoped that his rank and the letter of recommendation from his colonel would be sufficient for Sophia's father to at least consider him worthy of rejoining the estate. The people there were the only family he had left. He wanted to hug Mrs Gribbins and taste her wholesome baking, and then see his old friend Robert Judd. They had never even had the chance to say goodbye. At least he had been allowed to be escorted to the town by his father. He swallowed as he remembered their last parting. He missed him so much.

'I think perhaps you are being modest,' Lucas said. 'I, on the other hand, have not served. I am an only son of a self-made man who is planning to set up a life in a land far removed from the troubles over here. Not exactly the desires of a patriotic hero, but definitely the mind of a man who knows how to survive. However, I will not survive my father's wrath, if I do not find a way to make myself presentable and ride over to Fenton Hall tomorrow.'

'Fenton Hall?' Isaac stood up and winced in his haste. He suddenly looked at this man in a different light. He was a few years his senior, definitely able to pay his way, not ungainly in appearance and was preening himself ready to arrive at the Hall. Could this mean that his Sophia was promised to Huntley?

'You know of it?' Lucas glanced at Isaac; his curiosity obviously roused.

'Yes, I am going there tomorrow too, as

soon as I have arranged for some transport.' Isaac felt oddly vulnerable sharing this information. However, he was taken by surprise when Lucas Huntley immediately smiled back at him and clasped his hands together.

'Then it is settled! You must arrive with me tomorrow evening. Instead of a horse I shall rent a gig and you must come with me as my honoured guest. I shall send word on.'

'As your guest? Is that acceptable, or expected, sir?' Isaac asked him. He was tempted to go along with the man's request but was unsure if he would then make the entrance he hoped for, or if he might be shot in his good leg for his insolence at presuming he would be made welcome by Sir Kenneth.

'Oh, absolutely, I insist, man! And when a Huntley insists you should not question our generosity. You will be my guest. It is a position you have earned.' Lucas's attention turned to his attire. 'Now, I must look suitable.'

'Very well,' Isaac nodded and sat back

down. What had he to lose? He swallowed as he replaced the image of an irate Sir Kenneth with that of his loving and gentle Sophia.

Lucas swung around. 'Good man. You have turned what was to be a drag of a day into one more promising. We can pass some time at the auction before we attend.'

'I accept your kind invitation,' Isaac said.

'Good. I shall make enquiries and ready a gig. I will send that young lad over to let them know I intend to arrive with a war hero as a companion!' Lucas was positively animated.

Lucas left the room and Isaac heard his footsteps running down the wooden stairs two at a time. How he wished he could do that still.

What had he done? What if Sophia hated him now for nearly causing her ruin? Had he thought his return through at all?

The truth was he had nowhere else to go and he had been kept alive by the image of the young woman in his dreams to block out the nightmares of the death and mayhem around him. Sophia had been out of his reach before he left but now he had achieved his rank and commendation, maybe there was a chance. But would it be enough for Sophia or her father to accept him back? Would it ever be enough?

4

Lucas Huntley bounded down the stairs. What luck had fallen into his path! For Lucas to turn up at Fenton Hall instead of his father should be a pleasant enough surprise, unless gossip had travelled about his broken engagement. However, arriving with his newfound friend, the good lieutenant, would shine a different light upon him as the lieutenant would hardly be seen as someone who would keep company with a rogue.

Lucas peered through the crowd in the dim light and saw the young lad tucked into a nook by the fire. Lucas beckoned to the lad, who promptly came over.

'I need to send a message up to Fenton Hall. Do you know anyone who could arrange one there for me?' Lucas raised an eyebrow and put his hand in his pocket jangling his coin purse as if unconsciously doing so.

'Aye, I could, if Mr Pulley will let me

use one of his nags. He's in the tap room. You just wait here and I'll go ask him.' He dipped around the end of the servery and disappeared behind a swing door.

Lucas was not someone who liked being told what he should do or where he should wait, especially by a slip of a boy, so he made his way through the queue of men and crossed to the doorway where the lad had vanished from his sight. He leaned on it gently as he perched on an upturned barrel to one side. Using his boot he opened it an inch.

'What is it, Midge?' a voice asked.

'Sorry, Mr Pulley, for interruptin' but a man wants to get word to Fenton Hall tonight,' the lad explained.

'What sort of word?' another voice asked him.

There was a pause. 'Dunno!' the lad admitted.

'Bleedin' idiot! Why didn't you ask him?' Mr Pulley's voice boomed.

'I thought I could ride one of them nags over and be back before night falls proper. I didn't think he'd tell me it in words, Mr Pulley, so it would be written down. I guess he'd tell you though unless it be for his lordship, personal, wouldn't he?' The lad's voice was small by comparison.

The other man cut in, his voice not as angry and harsh as the man Pulley's was. 'Well, Midge, unless he was going to write it down he would have to tell you, wouldn't he, but seeing as I am returning shortly, you go back and find out this message and tell him it will be done. He need not know by whom, he may not even care.'

'Yes, I will, Mr Judd, thank you kindly.'

Lucas returned to where he had been left and waited for Midge to come back to him. Who it was in the tap room with the innkeeper he did not know, but as the man had rightly said as long as his message arrived he didn't care either way who delivered it. However, life had taught Lucas that it always paid to know more than any stranger thought you did about them. He wanted to know who this man Judd was who was interested in him.

'Mister, your message can be taken this night,' Midge said as he presented himself keenly in front of Lucas.

'Good lad,' Lucas said. 'I have not written it down, but can you tell them that Mr Huntley will be arriving with a guest, a newly returned hero, a lieutenant from the wars.'

'Is that it?' Midge asked.

'Yes, now you repeat it back to me.'

'Mr Huntley is arriving with his guest — a hero, a lieutenant just come back from the wars.' Midge looked pleased with himself.

'It's near enough. Here.' Lucas offered the lad a few coins for his trouble. 'I'll know tomorrow if the message got there or no, so if they are not expecting us on arrival then I will know where to come to get that coin back.'

'Midge will see it gets there right! I am as good as my word — folk here trust Midge.'

'Good man,' Lucas said.

When Midge had left, Lucas slipped

out of the inn and went around the back to the stables. He wanted to check on his wounded horse. He might also be able to glimpse this man Judd as he left.

Seeing that there was no one in the stables he slipped into the end stall from where he could see the entrance to the tap room at the back of the inn. When the door opened and the innkeeper and the man Judd came out, Lucas made his way down the stalls to his horse and kept himself out of view.

'So their party's finished and now they got more folk comin'?' The man called Pulley did not seem pleased. 'Not usual, is it?'

'Well, they have people now and then, but it doesn't affect me much unless they are going hunting and need the horses,' Judd replied. He was a dark haired wiry character, who looked as if he would have made a good jockey. 'Don't take on so, Jethro. They can afford to change their minds and we serve as best we can around their whims. It is the way of the world and will never change, so stop bemoaning it. Oh and see that Mrs Gribbins gets her supplies tomorrow as planned. She'll be low on stock after the party.'

Lucas heard a horse being walked out from the end of the row of stalls. He waited until they had left and made his way back to the room.

5

Isaac slept well. He was aware of the other man snoring but it was only when his leg was knocked that he awoke with a start. His heart immediately filled with joy despite his discomfort, for today he would return to Fenton Hall.

He swung his legs out of the bed and sat up. He used the cold water in the bowl on the side table to rinse his face. It felt fresh. Another ten minutes and he was dressed, with his hair combed and boots pulled on. He reached for his coat just as Lucas woke up.

'Wait on and I'll break my fast with you,' Lucas said. 'We'll leave the bags here and go and investigate this auction. I admire a bit of good horseflesh, don't you?'

Isaac nodded and eased his coat on. He had wanted to be able to take a stroll before the crowds built up and he would be jostled. Lucas was up, dressed and looking quite dapper in minutes, making Isaac realise just how long his own struggle had taken. How was he ever going to impress Sophia like that?

'C'mon man.' Lucas slapped Isaac's back as he passed him and opened the door. 'I'll go down and order whilst you make your way. No rush.' The words drifted on the air as Lucas disappeared from view.

The food was good and fresh. Fried eggs with thick, runny yolks on a chunk of ham and fresh bread. With enthusiasm, Isaac tucked in and washed it down with a decent ale. He suddenly felt more alert. 'So have you been here before?' Isaac asked Lucas.

'No, never. I doubt I'll ever be back here again. I'm only here because my father wishes me to attend Sir Baxter-Lodge on his estate.'

'Just friends then,' Isaac casually persisted.

'Sir Kenneth is a friend of my father's and I am going to negotiate a business deal on my father's behalf. Do you know the family?' Lucas asked.

'I have connections there. Sir Kenneth knew my father well. I wanted to pay my respects to him.' Isaac bent the truth with ease.

Lucas raised his tankard. 'To fathers, bless their souls,' he said, grinning broadly, though his manner did not seem genuine.

Once out in the milieu, Isaac looked around. Flocks of sheep were being driven up the road outside to be herded into pens by the market. A cart full of fresh bread was being pushed down one side of the road, followed by another with cheeses and eggs resting upon fresh hay and a load of tanned skins at the other side of the road was followed closely by a chandler carefully carrying a basket of his goods. Shouts went back and forth as people greeted each other.

As they approached the tolls for the sheep pen Lucas touched Isaac's arm and gestured to two Thoroughbred horses that were being ridden into the stall.

'Now they are worth looking at!' Lucas said. He tugged Isaac's sleeve. 'Come, man, let's see them close up.'

Isaac followed him some paces behind. He could see that Lucas was drawn to these racers like a moth to the light. He had seen gentry taken so before and he knew straight away that Lucas liked his bets. Was he a winner or a loser? Time would tell.

Whilst Lucas looked closely at the two beasts Isaac noticed with a jolt that Robert Judd was approaching. Isaac was not ready to reveal his return just yet, so he stepped away, losing himself in the crowd, but his heart lifted at the sight of his old friend.

Robert Judd walked up to a man by the horse's stall who he obviously knew well by the way they exchanged easy banter. It took much of Isaac's willpower not to call out to him, but he knew he would regret doing so. He did not want anyone at Fenton Hall to have prior warning of his return, especially Sir Kenneth and Sophia. This time he must arrive as a gentleman would, through the main door and not crawling back through the kitchens as a servant.

Robert gave the man something. The stranger shook his hand heartily and they parted. Isaac watched Robert walk over to a flower girl and buy a small posy. So, his friend had a sweetheart, Isaac though. Robert walked out of sight and Isaac stepped forward again to join Lucas.

'Let's find a good place to sit down and watch the bids begin.' Lucas pointed to the seating area.

'Will you bid for one?' Isaac asked.

'Heaven's no, but I am always interested in seeing the horses before a race meeting if they are due to run.'

'Are they?' Isaac asked.

'According to their groom they are down for the York event in two weeks. So whoever buys them could be buying a winner.'

'Or a loser,' Isaac said. He thought the chestnut lacked form, but the grey looked full of life. He knew his horses, but did Lucas?

'That man who came over to the groom seemed to know which would win or stand a chance. He liked the chestnut,' Lucas said.

'Which man?' Isaac asked, thinking he could not mean Robert for he would never make such a mistake.

'Did you not see him?' Lucas was obviously surprised.

Isaac nodded in the direction of a carriage with a pretty young woman seated on it, and grinned. 'I had my eyes on another filly,' he lied, and Lucas laughed, not doubting him for one minute.

'Oh, my poor hero, you would have to bring one of Napoleon's eagles home to net a catch such as she, unless your dear departed father had been a lord of the realm.'

'I cannot help but admire such beauty,' Isaac said, grateful to distract Lucas, yet he did not mean it. He only had eyes for Sophia.

The auction began with the fast banter of the bidding. It was a strange inaudible blur of language to any but the trained ear and yet Isaac knew it so well. Lucas looked excited as the highlights of the auction were brought into the ring. First in was the grey horse. The bidding went well. Lucas was on the edge of his seat.

'Well, whoever got that beast has a fine chance at York. I shall watch out for it.'

Isaac nodded and discreetly rubbed his leg. The chestnut was bid for as well, and then the auction ended.

Lucas left to see to his business and Isaac arranged to meet him back at the inn in a short while. Isaac walked along the flat pavements and then crossed the busy road, making his way into the churchyard. He had never before seen the grave he was looking for, but straight away he noticed the flowers Robert Judd had bought in the market laid on a nearby headstone. Isaac stepped forward and looked down.

The inscription was simple:

Here lieth the body of
Joshua Henry Dalesman

Much loved father of Isaac.
11th March 1748 — 15th April 1808

Isaac lost track of how many minutes he stood there, but when he moved his leg felt as though it had locked stiff. He straightened it out, painfully, and rubbed it until he could walk away again.

'Mr Huntley, I've found you at last!' A man in a worn tweed suit had rounded the church corner and was running towards Isaac. 'Don't try and flit off again.'

'I beg your pardon?' Isaac said. When he turned his greatcoat fell open and his uniform was plain to see.

'Damnation!' The man stopped, clearly disappointed.

'Words and place, sir,' Isaac snapped, as he gestured to the church and then glanced back at his father's grave. 'Who are you?'

'Sorry, sir. Philip Entwhistle. I was told a Mr Lucas Huntley was in town and that he went this way.' He sighed heavily. His colour was high from running.

'What do you want Mr Huntley for?' Isaac asked.

Entwhistle pushed his hand into his pocket and pulled out a letter. 'Do you know the man, sir? Is he near?' he asked.

'I might be able to locate him if you could tell me what the urgency is.'

Entwhistle handed the letter to Isaac.

Isaac read it with interest.

6

Sophia was staring at her reflection in the looking glass when Cynthia entered her bedchamber.

'My dear, you look divine,' Cynthia said. 'Our guests are going to be so impressed when they see you. You are the perfect image of a daughter of a family of standing and wealth. Your father will be so proud of you.'

'That will be a first,' Sophia said without thinking.

'Really, Sophia, that is unfair, untrue and beneath you!'

'My apologies, it was not meant.' Sophia smiled and quickly changed the subject. 'Our guests, Cynthia? I thought it was just Mr Huntley who was arriving?'

'So did I, but Brent informed your father that when Judd returned from Gorebeck he had been given a message that Mr Huntley would arrive with a recently returned lieutenant — a brave man said to have acted most heroically! So we shall be more entertained than entertaining, shall we not?' Her eyes were so bright that Sophia thought they absolutely shone.

'So what is the name of this man, whose reputation goes before him?' Sophia asked.

'That's the thing, Sophia, we have absolutely no idea.' Cynthia giggled in her girlish way. 'Judd, the stupid man, forgot to ask.' Cynthia stood at the side of Sophia staring into the looking glass. She began to correct one of her locks of hair that had gone astray. 'I must have this sorted out or I will look like the common farmer's wife next to the beautiful heiress!' she said fondly. 'I will go now and leave you to compose yourself. Do not dally long or you will have me all a dither greeting our mystery guests on my own. Oh, I do hope he wears a uniform — young officers do look so grand when dressed in their finery.'

Sophia laughed and shook her head as

Cynthia left to preen herself.

She took a few moments to acknowledge Cynthia's compliments — maybe she was quite pretty, despite having 'strong features'. Was it the diamond and sapphire necklace she had chosen to wear that made such a difference? She could see it brought out the deep sapphire blue of her eyes.

How strange it was that wearing fashionable clothes, like putting on a mask, could make such a difference. The immaculate curls that covered part of her forehead had been lifted higher so that she was crowned by a cascade of dark brown ringlets and the finely twisted gold band that held them in place was bejewelled to match her necklace. The golden threads that were woven through the sapphire ribbons complemented the floral embroidery on her matching silk gown, as it flowed down from the high waistline to the floor. The swoop of the low neckline supported her bosom and shapely waist. She must definitely have to remember to keep her back straight at all times lest she reveal the full curvature.

Oh, if only her Isaac could see her now! She closed her eyes briefly as she allowed an indulgent moment of a forbidden memory — Isaac's gentle touch. How alive the memory made her feel.

Her eyes opened abruptly as her father's threats echoed in her head, killing her moment of pleasure. How would her father ever understand that she was in love with Isaac? Would she be an old maid before her Isaac returned to her?

'Enough staring and lamenting,' she admonished herself. It was time to go and meet the guests. But first she must ensure her father approved of Cynthia's choice of dress for her. She hoped that he would be reminded that she was the daughter of the house and not his unpaid housekeeper.

Sophia approached his study door with mixed feelings bubbling away inside her, elation and foreboding jostling side by side. Taking a deep breath she walked purposefully into the room.

'Father,' she said lightly, closing the door behind her. She did not want Cynthia to swoop in and break her moment.

'What is it, Soph —?' Sir Kenneth's words stopped, drifting off into the space between them as he raised his head and saw her standing there.

She smiled. It had worked — he was definitely surprised. 'I wanted to know if you thought that I now looked appealing enough, Father?' she asked innocently and saw him swallow before he replied.

'You look quite stunning, my dear. In fact, for a moment I could have believed you were your mother — you are the image of her beauty.' He cleared his throat and stood up. His watery eyes refocused. 'You would make her very proud, as you have made me,' he added. He moved around the desk to stand before her. His light kiss on her forehead as his hands cupped hers was the most intimate gesture Sophia could remember sharing with him.

A knock on the door interrupted the moment.

'Yes!' Sir Kenneth's usual business-like tone returned.

'A gig is approaching, sir,' the butler, Brent, said, 'with two gentlemen riding in it. Mr Huntley and his guest, I presume, sir.'

'Very well,' Sir Kenneth said. Brent left them alone. Sir Kenneth nodded at Sophia. 'You are indeed appealing enough. Now, go to Cynthia, and make sure she is ready to greet our guests.' He smiled at her with genuine approval. 'Who knows, I may set Annabelle's needs aside and consider a match for you, instead.'

Sophia gave in to a childish impulse and hugged him, but she had no wish to be matched. Tonight would be her triumph. She would show how much she had matured and her father would revel in that and they would share a new respect for each other. She left with a happy heart, believing that they had truly put the past behind them.

7

Isaac's resolve began to falter as the gig pulled up outside the grand doors of Fenton Hall. This was not the view of it he was used to. He automatically felt as though he should take the horse and gig around to the stables. Should he have confided in Lucas that he had once worked here? No, that would be folly. He had plans that would be made clear in time. For now, all he needed to do was gain entrance and Sir Kenneth's good will — that was all.

'Well, it is certainly more than a farmhouse!' Lucas said as the gig pulled onto the long oak lined drive.

'Yes, it is far more than that,' Isaac acknowledged, realising just how grand the mansion was when approached from the main entrance. The effect of the white edge stones to its angular uniform build was to soften and contrast the vibrant red brick. The colonnades framing the entrance gave its simple lines a sense of grandeur.

Lucas secured the brake and stepped down as a footman steadied the horse. Isaac braced himself before standing and, carrying his cane, he carefully followed. The footman was unknown to him and so all he had to do was pass Brent without being recognised.

'Please come this way.' Brent gestured for them to go inside. He smiled at both of them, but Isaac had not been instantly recognised. Could it be because he was now a few inches taller, his muscle was that of a man and not a strap of a lad, his bearing was prouder and his uniform was a distraction? The lines on his forehead were etched out due to the visions seen of battle and he had intended to shave before the visit, but in the end he decided to trim his small beard, as he had become used to its feel. He hoped that it would be a barrier to separate the image of him as a lad, so Sir Kenneth would see him as a man who had matured and grown.

Lucas gazed around him as they passed between the two Grecian style columns that framed the doorway. Inside, it was obvious that the columns had been added on to the original facade, for the old oak that formed the great staircase ascended to a drawing room above. It had been designed so that a carriage could have entered the entrance hall for its passengers to alight in the shelter of their ornate home and then drive straight out the matching doors at the other side. The family had obviously accrued much wealth over many years.

'This place is like a mausoleum,' Luke muttered to Isaac, who was taken aback by his offhand comment. 'I half expect King Arthur to come riding out of the ancestral cellars on a white charger,' he said and chuckled.

Isaac stared around the open expanse of the hall; it was old, ancient stone standing as testament to the age of the building. Surely that past was something Isaac had been fighting to preserve in their present?

Isaac slowly moved forward, balancing his weight carefully, but his leg pains did not ease like they had earlier. He pushed the pain of his wound down deep and followed Lucas into the Hall. Isaac had never seen this part of the building; he had been limited to the servants' passages.

'Ah, Lucas!' Sir Kenneth Baxter-Lodge appeared at the top of the stairs with his arms raised to greet his guests. 'I was expecting your father but am delighted that you came in his stead.' He approached them. 'I hope all is well with him?'

'Yes, sir, he is fine and sends his apologies.'

Hearing Sir Kenneth's voice caused Isaac's already unsteady steps to falter further. He instinctively studied the tapestry next to him in earnest as he gathered his thoughts.

'Thank you for inviting us, Sir Kenneth,' Lucas replied, glancing down to see Isaac had momentarily halted.

'You are more than welcome, Lucas.

I thought for a moment that your father had found the elixir of youth!' He laughed heartily. 'Please, go inside.' He ushered Lucas through the open doorway into the drawing room.

Isaac thought that it was better that the initial shock of his arrival and possible ejection from the Hall should happen here, unseen and unexplained to his new friend, so he remained where he was standing.

'Any hero of our country is forever welcome in my home, Lieutenant.' Sir Kenneth's voice seemed to resound off the stone walls, or was it Isaac's own conscience that amplified those words? Last time they met Isaac had been told never to cross his path again. Yet here he was, a hero being greeted magnanimously in the main entrance of Sir Kenneth's home.

'Thank you,' Isaac replied, still plucking up the courage to look Sir Kenneth in the eye. He wondered if his leg would be up to another knock should he find himself thrown bodily back down to the entrance hall. He really had not taken sufficient time to think this through. He braced himself as Sir Kenneth approached him.

'I see you admire our family's taste in décor,' Sir Kenneth said as he walked down the few stairs to stand by Isaac's side.

Isaac could hear light chatter coming from the drawing room. Where was his Sophia? A thought made his blood turn cold — what if he was too late and she had been married off already? It would not be unusual; she was more than old enough and Isaac knew that her heart's desires would not be taken into account by her father.

Sir Kenneth continued, 'My ancestor Lord Broderick Baxter-Lodge acquired them in France around 1660, when serving as a representative of Charles II in Versailles. I should be able to bring to mind what it is about, but it has been so long since I really looked at them that I cannot remember. Strange, you pass them by daily like so many of the trinkets we possess, but I never stop and admire any of them. Oh, let the women understand and fuss about such things, I say. We men have estates to run, wars to fight, farming and industry to sort.' Sir Kenneth chuckled. 'So, where do you hail from, sir?' Sir Kenneth glanced down at Isaac fleetingly, but his eyes did not linger.

'Sir . . .' Isaac waited until he had the man's attention. He needed to look him in the eye and judge his response.

Sir Kenneth stared at Isaac's face, searching his features. He settled on his eyes. 'Have we been introduced before, sir?' he asked. 'You seem familiar to me, and yet I cannot quite place you . . . Perhaps we met last summer in Harrogate? Or York — the races perhaps — are you a gambling man? No, of course not, you are newly returned, so you wouldn't be there. Forgive me. Perhaps I know your father?'

'Indeed, we have met, Sir Kenneth, and you knew my father very well. The connection *is* actually through horses, your horses . . .' Isaac began.

Sir Kenneth placed a hand on his shoulder and gently turned him towards the drawing room. 'My manners are at fault here; you should come and enjoy my home. Any man who has returned a celebrated hero has many a story to tell I'll wager . . . and I want to hear them.' Kenneth made to move forward, but Isaac stood firm.

'Sir, it is I who owes you greatly, as does all my family, especially my poor father who passed away whilst I was serving. Joshua Dalesman was a true God-fearing man who served you well with love and dedication.' Isaac swallowed then quickly added, 'I owe you for seeing to his final resting place and I will repay you in full, Sir Kenneth. I have a letter of recommendation from my colonel who would ask that you reinstate me in a position of trust here, whilst I heal from my wound. I was injured in a battle: a bad fall trapped under a dying horse, and was fortunate to have survived . . .'

Isaac swallowed again, his mouth

becoming dry. Yes, he had fought in battles and nearly died, and yet he had never been as fearful as he was facing this man now. He wanted Sir Kenneth's respect, to be acknowledged as a man worthy of at least sitting at his table, if not the hand of his daughter — yet. The war was far from won and he would mend and return and climb higher up the ranks one way or another. If not by further merit then he would in time purchase a commission like a true gentleman could until he was sufficiently raised to be worthy of Sophia in her father's eye.

Sir Kenneth had stopped. 'What do you mean reinstate you here? Dalesman . . . You are that lad . . . Isaac . . .' The tone in his voice had changed and the air between them stilled.

'Yes, it is me, Lieutenant Isaac Dalesman. I served in the Light Dragoons to prove myself worthy of your forgiveness, and I hope the recommendation I carry speak to my character. I was very young when I left here, but I am a man full grown now who has saved my battalion from starvation.' Isaac could not read the emotion that was crossing Sir Kenneth's face. Was it shock, disbelief or rage?

Sir Kenneth just stared at Isaac.

Isaac cleared his throat. 'I see I may have made an error of judgement in accepting Mr Huntley's invitation.' Isaac tried to pull away from Sir Kenneth's grip, which was gradually becoming firmer. 'Perhaps I should have seen Mrs Gribbins first and entered at a time and place more befitting my origins.' Isaac looked down and began to gingerly edge his way around, ready to carefully descend the stairs.

'You have arrived here as my good friend's guest. As a hero! Tell me, does he know of your connection to the Hall?' Sir Kenneth asked quietly.

'No, sir, we are newly acquainted. I merely explained that I was to present myself here as I had a letter from my colonel and he insisted we arrive together.' Isaac looked directly at Sir Kenneth.

'Good, then he will remain here with you, and you will enjoy my food at my table. I take it you know how to behave in respectable company?' His eyes bore into Isaac's.

'Yes, sir,' Isaac answered honestly. He was not insulted as it was a fair comment to ask his once stable lad.

'Good! I will talk to you on your own once my business with Lucas Huntley is done. Do not do anything to sour it, my lad, or you will not enjoy being a hero for long!'

'Of course, Sir Kenneth,' Isaac said.

He felt the firm slap on his shoulder and realised it was harder than appropriate, but as he began to climb the last few stairs a vision of perfection waited for him at the top. Sophia appeared in the doorway of the drawing room and Isaac missed the top step and nearly tripped up. Sir Kenneth's grip held him upright, preventing Isaac from tumbling down into oblivion.

'Good God, man,' Sir Kenneth snapped. 'Compose yourself.'

'Yes, sir,' an embarrassed Isaac replied as he admired the beauty that Sophia had become.

'Mr Huntley, I was not aware you were in the army,' Sophia said innocently.

'He is not, Sophia,' Isaac responded and saw the instant recognition spread across her face.

'Isaac!' she whispered.

'Lieutenant Dalesman is Mr Huntley's guest, Sophia. You will act as if he is a stranger to you.'

'Yes, Father,' she replied. She nodded her assent, but Isaac had seen his Sophia's eyes shine brightly and her cheeks colour delicately. She was still his, but he hoped that her father was not as aware of this as he was. But could Lucas Huntley be the man Sir Kenneth intended as Sophia's betrothed?

8

Sir Kenneth led the way into the dining room. The table, which was normally extended to seat at least ten with ease, had had its middle section removed so that the two semi-circular ends had been joined to form a full circle. Five places had been evenly set upon a starched white tablecloth edged with Belgian lace.

'My dear Sophia, you never shy from breaking with convention, but for a very practical purpose. We shall be able to converse with ease,' Sir Kenneth said as he hesitated before taking the seat, which would have normally been at the head of the longer table.

'I cannot take the praise for this, Father. This is Cynthia's inspired arrangement.'

The ladies stood behind their chairs whilst two footmen slid them out so that they may be comfortably seated. Sophia held onto the back of the chair for a moment as she steadied her inner tremor. Isaac was here! Now!

Isaac and Lucas were shown their places and also sat down. The first plates of food were brought in, the exquisite display giving a promise of a very satisfying meal.

'I prefer to eat *à la russe*,' Cynthia explained, 'I find *à la française* so wasteful and awkward, don't you agree, Mr Huntley?' Cynthia asked and Sophia saw the look of relief on Isaac's face that he had not been addressed with the question. He may look every inch a gentleman, but she suspected he still had vast gaps in his knowledge of dining.

She blinked — no he had not vanished. This was no mirage or dream; her Isaac had returned to her. She caught Sir Kenneth's stern expression and diverted her attention to Mr Huntley, who appeared to be years younger than she had expected. Her father explained that this was Lucas Huntley, the son, and that Charles Huntley had been unable to attend.

'Indeed, but good food no matter how

it is served tastes divine anyway,' Mr Huntley replied. 'Of course the excellent company can only enhance the experience further,' he added and smiled at his hostess.

'Indeed! Indeed!' exclaimed Sir Kenneth as the plates were served.

Throughout the meal it was Mr Huntley who was the quieter of the two gentlemen as Sir Kenneth repeatedly asked questions of Isaac about the battles he had fought in. If he was angered by Isaac's presence he controlled it well. It was as if he was being cross-examined on his part in the conflicts so far, and on the state of the current situations.

Sophia secretly hung on his every word but tried not so much as to look in Isaac's direction for more than a cursory glance. The shock of seeing him again and in such a manner as to be eating with him at her father's table had not worn off. Surreal moments passed by as she tried to eat her food, yet she could not control her inner turmoil of emotions and excitement. Did this mean her father had finally accepted him? Had he known he was to join them? So many questions raced around her head and the desire to fling her arms around his neck was unbearably strong. She sipped her wine; it did not help.

Sophia asked Mr Huntley innocent questions about his preferences for the food, the state of the roads, his travels — anything to try and initiate a conversation that would engage his attention. She had heard the rumours of Mr Lucas Huntley breaking off his engagement. He may be very eligible but rumours had spread of his disreputable past. Was he a cad? If so, why was he being entertained at her father's table? And how had he come to know Isaac? Were the two men friends?

'Mr Huntley, I hope your father is well and that your presence here means that he is not unable to travel,' Sophia asked, turning to him trying to find anything out that may be of interest to her father.

'He has had to take his rest. Father works so hard and he caught a slight chill and needed time to recover. Travelling this far north would have been out of the question. I feel he needs to live in a warmer climate.'

'But how will he manage to traverse an ocean to Australia?' Sophia asked innocently.

'With ease, I am sure, for the climate will be warmer and sea air is such a good healer. Besides, he is yet strong. He has been running around visiting old friends and tying up business with his acquaintances. I already needed to travel to Newcastle and so it was my suggestion that I pop in here so he could regain his normal energy,' Mr Huntley explained.

'Very wise, and so thoughtful,' Cynthia said. She was being quite quiet, Sophia thought.

Sophia swallowed a sip of wine. It did little to clear her thoughts. Isaac had returned to her — here he was sitting at their table — her hero! Sophia was dressed to perfection to impress the wrong man. She ached to be alone with Isaac to find out why he limped and how, or if, he had changed from the sweet stable boy she knew. Surely war embittered men. Her father seemed to be dealing with the situation in a very calm manner. Unusually calm, she thought.

Despite Sophia's best efforts, she found the seating a little awkward; being placed between her father and Lucas Huntley. Cynthia had thought a round table would be more apt than that of a rectangular one because they were a group of five. It was unusual but meant that everyone in the small group could join the conversation with ease.

Isaac was sat across from Sophia. She was determined to keep her eyes from taking in every rugged and handsome feature of her long lost friend. It had to be the hand of fate showing them the way, or destiny carving out a new way forward for them. Her father seemed determined to hook Isaac's attention throughout their dinner and she hoped he noticed that she was doing as he bid and appealing to Mr Lucas Huntley as instructed.

'Our new venture has kept Father in London for longer than he had expected,' Lucas Huntley told her. 'He will of course be seeing you all before we depart to the new lands. He will make it a priority; of that I am sure.' Lucas smiled at her and raised a glass. 'To your beauty, Miss Sophia, the image of which will stay with me for my journeys to come,' he said and then turned to Cynthia. 'And to your exquisite taste, ma'am.'

Sophia blushed as Lucas sipped his wine. He looked at her over his glass, as he had frequently throughout the meal. She sipped her water instead of her wine as the atmosphere was becoming far too heady for her and Mr Huntley's flattery was quite intoxicating. One man poured honeyed words discreetly into her ear, whilst the other glimpsed her, longingly, whenever he could.

'What business brought you up here?' she gently persisted. Sophia was aware that her father was also glancing her way.

'Well, I had to go to Newcastle to seal up an old family business but then word spread of a beautiful lady who was the daughter of my father's good friend and I could not keep away any longer. I had to see this rare treasure for myself before you were discovered in a Grand Assembly, as surely you will be soon.'

Sophia blushed slightly and chanced a peek at Isaac. She noted he was not smiling at all at the latest comment made by Lucas Huntley. So he too listened attentively. Sophia was humoured by the compliment, but she was not taken in so easily by false praises. Cynthia adored being the centre of attention amongst the wives of their guests; Sophia did not.

'You are really too kind,' she said. 'So tell me, when do you leave for Australia?'

Her father interrupted before Lucas Huntley could answer her. 'Ah, my dear Sophia, you are not to worry on that score. I shall need to talk further to Lucas, so I insist that our guests stay with us a while. I will have your things sent for from the inn and have the gig returned. Isaac, you will take the opportunity to rest that leg of yours and I will have Dr Aimes sent for to make sure all is well.' Her father was not asking but telling these two young men what he expected to happen.

'That is very generous of you, Sir Kenneth,' Isaac said. He looked surprised.

'I shall read what the good colonel has to say about you in his letter of recommendation,' Sir Kenneth added. 'Then we shall talk again, individually and collectively. It looks as though your meeting, gentlemen, was most opportune.' He forced a smile but his eyes did not convey the same geniality, Sophia realised.

Lucas Huntley sat back. 'This has been a most remarkable meal. However, I would suggest that I take the gig back to town and settle my affairs there. But I would be happy to rejoin you in a couple of hours' time, if you do not mind my late return? I have a lame horse in the inn's stabling, and if I could borrow one of yours I would bring both back with me. Perhaps your stables would provide a better place for it to recover, whilst we continue discussing my father's proposal.'

'Very well,' Sir Kenneth announced and stood up. 'Brent!' he bellowed and the man appeared at the doorway. 'See that Mr Huntley has everything he needs to return to town this evening and speak to Judd and make sure they are ready to tend an injured horse on his return.'

'Very well, sir,' Brent said, still apparently oblivious as to who Isaac actually was.

'I will be back before you miss me.' Lucas Huntley stood up, excused himself to Cynthia then turned to Sophia and smiled sweetly down at her.

He was certainly confident, she thought. Cynthia escorted him out.

Three people were left seated at a half empty table looking at each other with a growing silence forming between them.

'You must excuse me, Father, for I must withdraw.' Sophia decided to break it first. Leaving seemed the best option, lest she said the wrong thing so soon after Isaac's arrival.

'Stay here, Sophia,' her father ordered and her eyes locked fully with Isaac's for the first time since they had sat at the table. She hoped that all could be well between them, but those hopes were crushed when she saw her father's stern expression.

'You two are nothing to each other. Do I make myself clear on this matter? I will have this understood now, or one of you will leave tonight — and an untended injury, Isaac, could result in you being a lifelong cripple . . .'

Sophia gasped. 'Father!'

'Shush, child! Isaac has earned my gratitude for the way he has bettered himself and served his country, and for those reasons he shall be tended to. But you are an heiress and you, Lieutenant, are below her rank. I do not want history to repeat itself. That would result in your expulsion from this home with immediate effect, Isaac. Much as I love you, my daughter, I will not excuse such betrayal again ever. Do not break my trust in this either of you! If I find out that this was some ploy to fool me then I will banish you both.'

Sophia knew this was no idle threat and she could tell Isaac also understood that by the crestfallen look in his eyes.

'It is no ploy, Sir Kenneth,' Isaac stated. 'Sophia had no knowledge of my return and I met Mr Huntley by chance, as I explained.'

'You may go, Sophia,' her father declared and sat back in his chair as she departed without further word.

Once Sophia had left, Sir Kenneth turned once again to Isaac. 'Isaac, I want you to walk straight again, so I will pay for your leg to be given the best of attention. I owe it to my country, if not to you personally, and to your father's memory for as children we played together on this land and I would not go to my grave knowing I had let his son become a cripple. You were young and foolish once. I do not condemn you for following a young heart and an immature infatuation, but Sophia is not a simple farm wench. You must see that this infatuation cannot be rekindled. I shall find you a suitable bride if you so wish, in time. I can find you a lady who would be normally beyond your grasp. With my name behind you, doors can be opened.'

Isaac nodded. 'I am not playing you false, Sir Kenneth, but it is more than I deserve. You have my undying gratitude for the respect you show me, and I am not so foolish as to destroy the woman I love. This Hall is my home, as much as I ever had one. However, I will not burden you with finding a match for me. I will marry for love, or I will not marry at all.'

Isaac stood up, but his leg had had enough and it nearly buckled under his weight.

'Good God, man! You are suffering so much and still you do not say.' Sir Kenneth shook his head whilst patting Isaac's shoulder. 'Brent! Judd!'

A flustered Robert Judd arrived. 'Mr Brent has just left the building, sir. I'll fetch him; he was going toward the stables.'

'Yes, yes, I know that. He was looking for you. Get a couple of men and have Lieutenant Dalesman carried to his room. Make haste and send for the doctor.'

Isaac and Robert Judd's eyes locked momentarily as his friend mouthed silently 'Lieutenant Dalesman' before he turned and left.

Cynthia, who had returned when Sir Kenneth shouted for the servants, stood watching as Isaac held onto the edge of the table as he lowered himself carefully back into the chair. He had not realised until he moved how much was wrong with his leg. He had become used to the constant nagging pain, but now it could not bear his weight. The word 'cripple' resonated in his head. What use would he be to any woman if this was so? Certainly Sophia would forever remain out of his reach.

'Cynthia,' Sir Kenneth said, 'when the men arrive have Isaac lifted in the chair carefully up the stairs to the Willow room.'

9

The gig was waiting for him when Lucas Huntley stepped outside of the Hall.

'I need a horse as well to ride back with my injured one,' Lucas told Robert Judd.

Brent's voice was heard bellowing out from the Hall. 'Judd!' He appeared in the doorway. 'You're needed.' Brent did not wait for a reply but darted back inside.

Robert Judd shook his head.

'Looks like you have more than one role here,' Lucas said and noticed a flash of anger cross Robert Judd's dark eyes. 'Stables or Hall, which do you serve in?'

'Both, sir. I'll fetch the horse. I already have it saddled.' He turned and ran back around to the stable yard and then reappeared moments later with the horse.

'Judd!' the voice bellowed again.

'You had better go, Judd, before he bursts a lung. My thanks, she's a fine animal.' Lucas looked appreciatively at the horse.

'Sir Kenneth has a fine stock and I look after them well,' Robert Judd said as he ran up the steps.

Lucas drove the gig away with the spare horse being led on a long rein behind. Lucas liked horses and betting on the same. 'You were born a lucky bastard and that is no lie!' Lucas said to the wind, believing that his luck had changed. Miss Sophia was more comely than any farmer's daughter. Sir Kenneth's estate was also far grander than he had imagined. Perhaps he would be able to secure a wife and an inheritance before leaving England's shores. 'Oh Lucas,' he muttered to himself, 'can good fortune have smiled upon you at last?'

This was a feeling he had not experienced for nearly a year — happiness. Lucas was convinced he had just met the woman he would marry and take with him to Australia. His mind was set on it. Sophia was not only attractive, but she seemed to have some substance to her, speaking as if she had a brain and not just like some empty-headed parlour room gossiper.

Sophia seemed to be of a stronger breed than his Mary had been and Lucas was sure she would cope with the long journey and the harsher lifestyle awaiting them across a turbulent ocean. He needed a wench who could behave like a lady, but who would not faint when faced with the realities of life. Sophia had survived in the backwaters of Yorkshire and knew what a sheep was. Besides, her dowry would come in very useful.

Sophia was an only child and when Sir Kenneth joined his ancestors, the estate of Fenton Hall would be his to sell off. It would go for a decent price and that wealth would add to his estate in the colonies. Today was indeed a fortuitous one, for him and for Sophia. Without his help in rescuing her she would die an old maid in a grim and forgotten part of the world. Miss Sophia Baxter-Lodge should be exceedingly grateful for her good fortune.

Lucas could finally make up for the troubles of his past engagement. He was lucky not to have been thrown into prison for breaking his promise, and he was seen in the eyes of society as a rake and rogue. He smirked; it was a label that appealed to him anyway. It made him more effective in business dealings — appearing to be a more formidable character than he really was. When a debt had to be called in he gave a hint of menace to one of his debtors and miraculously they paid their dues. Besides, who would care about a broken engagement in the society where his destiny was headed? In his new life he would be a master of all; new money would become the established gentry — a fresh start, with the beautiful Sophia to sweeten any deal at a dinner party and grateful female servants to show their master their favour for a decent home and living. Lucas's family would get away from the stench of old money and begin a new dynasty where the sun shone with real warmth and bitter winters were miles away.

He breathed in the country air deeply. Lucas had thought he would have to pick a girl from the lower ranks, still fresh and hardy, but now he could see that would have been folly and left him open to further derision and ridicule if it became known amongst the army officers out there. His path was set, his mind made up — he would spend a week or two wooing Sophia and toying with Sir Kenneth, and then he would make sure Sophia was part of the business deal.

Lucas rode the vehicle back to the inn and settled his debt there, gave the gig back to its owner and collected his bag and the injured horse. He was keen to return to Fenton Hall as soon as possible.

This new turn of events was more fortuitous than he could have imagined. Like his new friend, he would become a hero; he would rescue Sophia and take her far, far away. At last he would not be a disappointment to his father. He glanced at the Norman church and chuckled as he left Gorebeck. What was he thinking?

Was he beginning to believe in God, or was he just seeing opportunity and taking charge of his own destiny? He smiled and carried on. It was the latter, for what God lets his minions die in such numbers on foreign soil as happened daily now? He kicked the horse on to a gentle trot to hasten his good fortune along and secure his future.

10

Isaac flinched in agony as he was moved up the stairs balanced upon a chair, carried precariously upwards by Robert Judd and another footman. If it had not been so painful it would have humoured him greatly to have been so ceremoniously lifted up the main stairs of Fenton Hall by his old friend. Every jolt sent a sharp pain down his leg.

Once in the beautifully decorated room, he was hoisted onto a four-poster bed. He closed his eyes as his body finally stilled, but the paralysing pain continued. He was sweating profusely and he stifled the urge to cry out when he landed on the bed.

To his embarrassment, a tear threatened to escape his closed lids — pray God he could not be crippled! No, not that! His panic had to be controlled and subdued. He felt like a frightened child, but he was a man and men were not supposed to cry. Something had definitely gone wrong with his wound. It was all he could do not to weep openly at the thought of losing his limb. He realised his imagination was running out of control and becoming wild, filled with visions of gloom. That was not like him. He breathed deeply, evenly, and then opened his eyes once the threat of moisture overwhelming them receded.

As he looked up abstractedly at the golden yellow drapes, he admired the work that had gone into their pattern, creating the effect of cascading leaves of a willow tree. They were beautiful, but he could not help but think they were weeping for him. Life was cruel, he knew that. His father had taught him that you just had to work hard and get on with it. He had fought tirelessly, ignored the prejudice from those who were against raising anyone up from the lower ranks, and tried to be hero enough for his Sophia — yet right now he was laid abed, broken with the cold threat of her father's words echoing in his head. It hurt, they all did: his leg, his heart and the memories that he did not wish to see anymore when he closed his eyes, of the canons blasting and men screaming.

'We have sent for the doctor, Lieutenant.' Cynthia's soft voice drifted into his thoughts and he glanced into her caring eyes. She had a delicate and concerned face.

'Sorry, I . . . Thank you for your kindness.' He saw her features relax as she obviously thought he had slipped off into deeper oblivion.

'I will ask Judd to see to your . . . to make you comfortable and change you into . . . so the doctor will be able to look at . . .' Cynthia nodded at his leg.

The poor woman was all of a fluster. Isaac wondered how she had come to marry Sir Kenneth. Lady Cynthia was pretty and gentle of manner, whereas Sir Kenneth was sturdy as a rock.

'Judd!' she called out.

Robert was only a step behind her and when he responded with a 'Yes, ma'am,' she moved to the side of the bed. She ordered him to make sure Isaac was made comfortable and change him as needed. She nodded at Isaac and quickly left them alone together.

Once Robert closed the door, Isaac stared at his old friend — they were both now men full grown and he had to hold back a flood of emotions as he felt the full force of the lost years of companionship.

Robert stared back at him. 'You never said goodbye, my friend.' The awkward silence was broken when Robert laughed. 'Sir Kenneth and your pa had your backside off this estate before I even returned from town.'

'It was like a blur, Robert.' Isaac shook his head. 'A nightmare I never want to relive. Sir Kenneth gave my father a note to present to the barracks and my life was changed overnight.'

'You survived, though,' Robert said and then looked at Isaac's leg before adding, 'Just.'

'I had to. I had to get back here,' Isaac said and Robert walked over to his side.

'Why? You are too late to see your father? Or do you still have designs on Miss Baxter-Lodge? If so, you are reaching for the stars.' Robert stared at Isaac. 'Surely you must see that, man. Even if you are a Lieutenant, hero, martyr, lover of damsels beyond his reach . . .'

'I'm not dead yet, Robert,' Isaac replied.

'You will be, my man, if you dare touch Miss Baxter-Lodge again.' Robert's face was full of mischief as he raised both eyebrows at Isaac.

'I know that.' It was something he did not need reminding of. 'Besides I never . . .'

'Good, because you have managed to leave with a boot behind your backside and yet here you are all cosy in the Willow guest room.'

'Not so cosy. My damn leg. Bloody hell, Robert, it hurts so.' Isaac was honest with him, as they had been such close friends as boys and he wanted to rekindle that brotherly friendship.

'Calm yourself, we have sent for the

local butcher.' Robert winked.

'Don't joke like that . . .' Isaac muttered. 'Not about my leg, please . . .'

'Very well, I shall not add to your pain, my long lost friend. You have risen far, but not high enough for Miss Baxter-Lodge.'

'Where did she come from — Sir Kenneth's wife?' Isaac asked, ignoring Robert's comments.

'That fine lady has been here for nearly four years and is a breath of fresh air. Sir went to London and came back with a wife. She is as light as a feather in character — good though. I'll not hear a bad word against her. We all feel protective of her because she brings this mausoleum to life. Now, let's get you changed and see if you are a wounded soldier or an amputee to be.'

His words cut through Isaac's heart like a sabre. 'Robert! Don't ever say that!' Isaac snapped, thinking how strange that Robert should have used the same word as Lucas to describe the Hall. Isaac saw the place as a testament to time and change. They only looked upon the old.

Robert nodded. ‘Sorry, I guess I’m just a little jealous of you. Here’s me running around passages like an invisible mole and serving the great and the good and you are out there being feasted as a hero.’ Robert shrugged and very carefully pulled off Isaac’s boot. ‘But I would not wish them to take off your leg. I am not that jealous or cruel.’ He winked at Isaac. ‘I always like to tease, but I’m only playing with you.’

Isaac nearly screamed out as the boot was removed from his injured leg. Once his breeches had been cast off it was clear to see that the bruising and swelling needed attention. Isaac was relieved, though, to see that the injury was all a mixture of healthy colours.

‘That knee looks mighty angry and not quite right in shape.’ Robert shook his head as he continued to remove Isaac’s uniform and give him a wash down before slipping a nightshirt over his head. Isaac had two scars on his back where he was almost cut down by a sabre in his first year of serving his king. They were old and healed, but still red and angry in comparison to the skin that covered the rest of his muscular back.

'What sights you must have seen, young Isaac, and all for the love of a woman.' Robert seemed genuinely surprised by Isaac's scars. 'I don't think I would go through this for a wench, no matter how comely or grand.'

'Aye, man, she is a good woman, who I still love,' Isaac confessed. 'Besides, it was good to do something where I felt needed and was able to perform well.'

'Oh, Lieutenant Dalesman when have you not done everything well?' Robert scoffed.

Isaac looked up, surprised at Robert's comment. 'I was caught in a tryst and have been nearly killed twice, for starters,' he said.

'Yes, but you had the love of a fancy young lady and lived twice when you could have been killed. So why did you return, especially as your father has long gone?' Robert looked down at this, his features showing genuine sadness.

'This is the only home I have known and I gave Sophia my word I would. I had to return and see if she was still my Sophia.' Isaac's voice was hardly audible.

'Then you are a doomed man, if not by Sir Kenneth when he realises you are undeterred, then by your stupid feelings of honour that may take you rejected and broken-hearted back to the fray,' Robert replied as he picked up Isaac's boots. 'I'll have these cleaned.'

'Robert, find out what you can about this Lucas Huntley chap. If he is being considered as a match for Sophia then I need to know,' Isaac said.

'You always were a dreamer. I'll do what we servants do best, young sir: listen silently as we blend in with the furniture.' He laughed. 'Remember to call her Miss Baxter-Lodge at all times, young sir. You are no more than an underling here — even as a lieutenant!'

'Very good, you may go, Robert,' Isaac said. Robert gathered up Isaac's uniform and left with a polite bow.

11

Sophia retired to her bedchamber, leaving Cynthia in the withdrawing room, resting on a chaise longue. When she had arrived at Fenton Hall, Cynthia had ordered one to be placed in each of her favourite rooms in the Hall so that she could relax after socialising.

With every moment that passed by, Sophia's anxiety grew. Her anticipation of seeing Isaac and speaking to him was stronger than the fear of her father's warning. Yet she dare not be caught, for that would have devastating consequences for Isaac.

She tiptoed to the banister and stared down beneath. The upper landing was directly above the main stairs to the dining and withdrawing rooms. Her father had left his study. Sophia stepped back and waited to see if he was going to come up the stairs but she heard Cynthia call out, so Sir Kenneth joined her and closed the door behind him.

Sophia decided she had stayed away from Isaac as long as she could stand to and she entered his room secretly through the servants' door that blended in with the wall.

'Isaac?' she whispered.

'Sophia.' He tried to prop himself up but flinched and remained where he was.

'You are badly hurt?' she asked, as she tiptoed across the room to be at his side.

'No . . . not really badly . . . just a bit.' He chuckled as he realised he was speaking as though placating a child — unconvincingly.

'You risked all to come back here to me. Oh, Isaac, you are so brave,' Sophia said, grasping his hand.

'Are you still true to me, my Sophia? I promised you I would come back, didn't I?' Isaac smiled and squeezed her hand. She looked sadly down into his weather worn face. The tanned, clear skin that she remembered was now bristled and worldlier, which she found even more becoming. The naivety of youth had been replaced with the features of a man — a handsome one, she thought.

'You have risked your health, your poor leg, to return to me and yet nothing has changed,' she said as she squatted at the side of the bed, so that her head could be near his and their voices, so quiet, could not be heard beyond the room.

'Oh, you are wrong — a lot has changed and it will still further, Sophia. I cannot ride a horse at present, and I am a guest in your home, honoured by your father. I have eaten at your table, met your new mama . . .'

'Don't call her that! She is Cynthia, Father's wife.' Sophia's snappish response silenced Isaac momentarily.

'Very well,' he said. 'I have been promised the services of a good doctor and that buys us time, because, if my leg can be fixed, it means we may well have a future together. Time is needed for Sir Kenneth to know me as the man I am now and for me to gain his acceptance.' He stroked her upper arm gently with his right hand and she wanted more than anything to melt into his embrace and stay there until morning. She was shameless where her Isaac was concerned, she knew that, but she was not so selfish as to risk him further injury from what would certainly be her father's inconsolable wrath.

'But we cannot be together, Isaac; he will still not allow us our happiness. Surely he must realise that our relationship is God-given? Why else would you have been guided into the company of Mr Huntley? It is just too much of a coincidence to have happened by pure chance. Yet, even after you giving so much to protect us . . .' Sophia's frustration felt overbearing and she had to struggle to control her voice for she could scream with despair at the cruelty of their fate. Her feelings were driven by a deep sense of injustice coupled with an equally strong feeling of helplessness. They were so near to each other, reunited, and yet her father's will and this awful injury separated them by miles.

'Then for now you must stay away from here, Sophia. Disappear back from where you came and be patient because I promise I will not burden you by being a cripple. If that is my destiny, it is not one that I will share with you.'

Sophia placed both hands at either side of his neck and leaned over him. She saw his eyes widen but ignored the playful glint. 'Isaac, I promised I would wait for you and I have. Not a day has passed by without me praying for your safe return, and here you are. In marriage we will promise to look after each other in sickness and in health, Isaac . . . I am not so fickle that . . .'

His hand shot up to silence her, his forefinger placed gently in front of her lips. Sophia kissed it, but he shook his head.

She stood back.

'Sophia, a man should start that marriage able in all aspects of life to support his wife and children. My body needs time to find strength and I have to think of a way to gain your father's approval. I have business matters to discuss with him, which may yet sway his mind in our favour, but it will never do so if you are found in my bedchamber. So I beg you, please leave! Be patient. I want you, Sophia, more than I ever have, but we must hold onto that faith of yours and bide our time. Oh and try not to become engaged to anyone else who happens to dine here!' He added the last comment and watched her eyes carefully. They had been moistening with concern, painfully and obviously pitying him. But when he spoke those last words her eyes sparkled. Good, Lucas had not snatched her attention yet. Her heart was still his to win or keep.

'I will never do that! I always knew you would return, but you must also stay strong, Isaac. Do not doubt my love and believe me when I say that you will never be a 'cripple' in my eyes. I shall go now.' She slipped back into the corner of the room's shadows and disappeared from sight as if she was a spirit of the night. If he had not felt a cold waft of air as she opened the passageway door, he could have believed she had come to him in a dream.

Isaac vowed he would not go to her lame. No matter how noble her words were, he would not spend a life being nursed and pitied. He would come to her in good health or not at all!

12

The next morning Sophia anxiously watched Dr Aimes arrive in her father's carriage. She wanted to be there to greet him, so ran down the stairs two at a time. Cynthia saw her approaching and discreetly placed her arm in the crook of Sophia's, stopping her from descending the final flight of stairs in such a rushed manner. Cynthia shook her head, a warning to Sophia to behave more as befits her station.

Brent opened the doors instead and let Dr Aimes in. Sir Kenneth strode out of his study and led the doctor up the staircase.

Sophia felt Cynthia's arm drop to her side, but only to slip her fingers around her own. Sophia looked at her.

'Do not worry, dear,' Cynthia said. 'Doctor Aimes is a man who has many years of experience behind him. He'll see that your lieutenant is well and walks straight again.' She squeezed Sophia's hand gently and Sophia acknowledged the kindly gesture, wondering how she had come to decide Isaac was 'her lieutenant'. Surely her father had not shared her past indiscretion with Cynthia?

Cynthia was sweet and she never wished anyone harm. If she knew how Sophia's heart ached at that moment to be there for Isaac then surely she would let her run up the stairs and not stand in her way? Sophia's mind was cast back to when the same two men had barred her from entering her mama's bedchamber. Anger burned inside; she was a woman now and Isaac would not leave her — he would be hers again.

'We must wait in the morning room. Your father will join us there. We cannot do more, dear Sophia,' Cynthia's voice whispered as she gently led Sophia away. 'Best not to get in their way; it would not be appropriate, dear.'

'I am only concerned for our guest's wellbeing.' Sophia held her head high and walked ahead so that her face would not reveal her inner turmoil. 'He is so young and I just hope the leg has not gone bad,' Sophia explained, hoping that she sounded convincing.

'I can see you are concerned for him, Sophia. Perhaps you should not let your father see how much you are, not yet anyway. I wouldn't want him to think that it was more than just Christian concern that filled your heart.' Cynthia's words made Sophia glance directly at her face. Cynthia scrunched up her nose and then winked at her. 'We must be a little more discreet if you wish to be allowed to talk with the young man whilst he convalesces. Patience will win the day!'

'Why ever would I wish to do that?' Sophia remarked defensively. Her words were a little sharper than she meant them to be.

'Because he is your friend, my dear, but whatever he was to you, if he is to be it again you are going to have to be very careful about the path the two of you walk. Take my advice. When a man's heart is set, he will do anything to get what he wants. You must protect your lieutenant from Sir Kenneth, but when a woman wants something against a man's will then she has to take the time to figure out how best to allow that man to change his will to fit hers. It is not easy, and it requires patience and cunning, but it can be done.'

Sophia looked at her stepmother. 'Why, Cynthia, I am surprised that you would give me such excellent and worldly advice,' Sophia said, admiring the deeper thinking that went on behind Cynthia's equally seemingly 'shallow' persona.

'Of course I am able to give you worldly advice, Sophia. I have lived in this world longer than you and have survived a father who died all too soon, a mother who remarried badly and a brother who would have gambled our complete fortune away. I know the weaknesses of mankind and have managed to survive quite well, thus far. My dear Kenneth is a man I love and admire beyond the stars, but he knows how ill fortune nearly destroyed my family and our good name.'

She placed her hands in her lap. Sophia had no knowledge of Cynthia's past and she realised that Cynthia must trust in her to be able to share it so openly now.

'Please explain then how you came to bring so much affluence to our own fortunes, Cynthia?' Sophia was amazed by the woman's ease of revelation and she wanted to know so much more. Her father had never disclosed how they met.

'Why, it was a simple solution once I found the right man, and your father was that because he is above all else fair and honest. I got him to gamble in a game of cards with my brother knowing that Kenneth would win easily. You see, Kenneth is a patient man and a strategist and I knew my brother's gaming faults. Your father thinks things through; he is not impulsive like my brother. My brother lost the family fortune on a bet to your father and, with it, me as part of the bargain. If it was not for Kenneth's generous spirit, dear Simeon would be languishing in Newgate Prison as a debtor and I would be having a life worse than a dog, but dear Kenneth loves me and I him. If we had not already fallen in love I would be a stranger's wife. Instead, I am perfectly happy with my life, I have a lovely daughter who is already grown up, and my brother is in Edinburgh studying medicine. If he fails to keep up with his studies, Kenneth will disown him. I believe he has made him a better man for this experience.'

Sophia stared blankly at Cynthia for a moment, for she had not called her 'daughter' to her face before. However, the word 'mother' would not form on Sophia's mouth by return. 'Why tell me all this now, Cynthia?' Sophia asked.

'Because you should know it. I have wanted to explain all to you for long enough, but it takes time to truly understand and grow in love with someone as you discover if you can trust them. Your father said I should judge the time right for myself, and I have. It is right now . . .' She patted Sophia's right hand between her two.

Sophia had never realised that whilst

she was feeling magnanimous accepting Cynthia into her home and sharing her father's life with her, her step-mother was going through a similar emotional acceptance of her. Sophia felt that she had been quite arrogant and now was somewhat humbled.

'You think you love this Isaac, but do not sell yourself short, my dear. Lucas Huntley is very handsome and attentive; he has money and is embarking on a very daring and exciting future. Before your fate is determined by men, know your own mind. I would suggest that you look at these two fine specimens of manhood and decide who is deserving of you. Of course, one is indisposed at the moment, but he hopefully should recover fully. They will both be here for a while. So, we shall see who wins, or deserves your affections, or if either or both fails to measure up.' Cynthia smiled at Sophia's shocked expression.

The doors swept open and Cynthia instantly put a hand on Sophia's knee to stop her from standing up in anticipation of news about Isaac's condition.

'Ladies, I am sorry that I took so long returning yesterday that I missed your company.' Lucas Huntley smiled apologetically. 'What news of our wounded hero?'

Sophia tried not to look disappointed at Lucas's appearance.

'I rose early,' Lucas Huntley continued, 'seeing to the wellbeing of my horse, who I am assured will be healed by your man Judd, who seems to understand the animals. The beast will make a full recovery with rest and care, so I wondered if I may enjoy your hospitality for a week whilst the wound mends?'

Cynthia smiled at him politely. 'We would be delighted to have you stay, wouldn't we, Sophia?'

Sophia dutifully nodded. 'I am delighted to hear that the horse will mend, Mr Huntley,' Sophia replied.

'So, how is our wounded soldier?' Lucas Huntley asked, looking from one to the other.

Sophia shook her head. 'We await my

father to bring us news of Lieutenant Daleman's situation. They have been up there for some time,' she said, trying to keep an even voice as her distress grew. She had seen soiled cloths being brought down and fresh water and dressings taken back up by Robert Judd and the maid. It was all too reminiscent of the day when her life changed from pampered, spoilt daughter with a doting mother, to one of cold, bone chilling loneliness.

'Thank goodness you have returned to us safely, Mr Huntley,' Cynthia said.

'Yes, though our man upstairs seems to be having a hard time of it. It must be dashed painful for a man like him to scream so. I do hope it can be saved.'

'What can be?' Sophia felt her head lighten as she stared back at him. Was he inferring that his leg may be forfeit, or his life?

'His leg, my dear Miss Sophia. He is young and strong but he may have to face the future as a man who walks with an uneven gait, but once on horseback again no one will ever know, unless he is unable to ride. I'm afraid so many of our wounded heroes return lesser men than they were before the conflicts.'

At that moment Sophia hated him — his hurtful words — his brutal honesty. It was a truth that should have remained unspoken. She did not think his words were needed at all.

Cynthia let out a gasp.

'My apologies,' Lucas said, realising his comments were indelicate.

'Poor man,' Cynthia whispered. 'He is so brave . . .'

'We should be hopeful that he will ride again in time,' Sophia said; her demeanour was covering up the inner turmoil that had threatened to undo her moments earlier. She had to stay strong, for Isaac's sake.

'Of course, of course,' Lucas agreed. 'We should always wish for the best outcome. I am certain that the doctor's skills will be better than any who serve in the field.' Lucas looked at Sophia and smiled. 'Still, a limp is nothing. In fact, it can be quite endearing for a gentleman,

I am sure. Just think of the ladies' heads he could turn at assemblies with tales of his bravado.'

Why was he labouring this point? Sophia wondered. Was it some sort of test of the depth of affection she had for Isaac? No, of course not — this man did not know that the two had ever met before. Sophia realised that her anxiety was leading her mind astray. Mr Huntley's bluntness would serve him well in the new lands, she was sure, but here he was becoming rather overbearing.

Cynthia stood up abruptly. 'I shall order hot chocolate for us all; would that be suitable for you, Mr Huntley?' Cynthia forced a polite smile at him; Sophia had learned to tell the subtle differences in Cynthia's facial expressions. She did not approve of Mr Huntley's comments either. 'I find a cup of it so very calming and all this excitement is getting a little over dramatic I feel.'

'Yes, yes, dear lady, of course. It would be just the thing. I left my bag in the hall,' Lucas said, and took a step to follow

Sophia as she summoned the house-maid.

Cynthia patted the sofa next to her where Sophia had been sitting. 'Sophia will see to it. She is so good at that. In fact, dear Sophia is gifted in whatever she turns her hand to. Do please keep me company whilst we wait for further news of Lieutenant Dalesman.'

Cynthia's comments, Sophia realised, were inconsequential. The woman was weaving a plot to keep Mr Huntley there whilst Sophia escaped. She happily left the room.

13

'What have you done?' Isaac asked after Robert Judd finally released his arms. A board had been placed under his leg, secured by ankle tethers, so that his body was held rigid. He could not jerk around as the doctor worked his ways. It was the most terrified Isaac had been in his life.

Isaac had been plied with an opiate — laudanum, he suspected — but, even so, the pain had passed through the haze, bringing him back to consciousness. He remembered hearing screaming; he was shocked on realising that it was his own. For a moment Isaac had been looking down on his own form in the room, seeing his body held there, helpless to fight back, and yet he was detached and above it all. The drug must have addled his senses, for it had all felt so real.

Isaac's vision was not as clear as it should be, but he anxiously stared around the room, then leaned over to peer at the floor by the bed where there was no sign of masses of bloodstained bedding, or his detached limb. The doctor was instead replacing his jacket and did not look like he had butchered a pig, so hope returned to Isaac's pulsing heart. He breathed deeply, knowing that he had survived the ordeal intact.

Isaac inched his hand slowly down his right thigh. As far as he could reach, he still had a leg, but he had no feeling in his foot — was it simply so cold that it was numb? He should not cry but he felt inclined to.

'Fortunately for you, Dr Aimes served on HMS *Royal Sovereign*, under Admiral Collingwood at Trafalgar, no less. Two heroes grace my house this day,' Sir Kenneth said with genuine pride.

'Please, Sir Kenneth, you are too kind.' The doctor seemed to revel in the praise.

Isaac did not feel like joining in their reverie. All he wanted to know was had he survived this ordeal — as a whole man?

'No, I say it as it is, Archibald. Despite

stooping to participating in the war as a mere surgeon, he learned a great deal from the experience, didn't you, Archibald?' Sir Kenneth asked his friend.

The use of the word 'surgeon' only served to scare Isaac further.

'You exaggerate, Sir Kenneth, I helped with the wounded from the vessel.'

'Same thing, same thing!'

'Perhaps you think so, but I wasn't actually on the vessel itself,' Dr Aimes said. 'Sometimes from the horror of war new progress is made through circumstance. It gives one the opportunity to learn on the job, as it were. You have to be bold enough to try new techniques. Some work, some do not, but in each case there is much to learn. And then future patients can benefit back home.'

Isaac swallowed. He felt pity for the poor sailors who the man had learned so much from. The man made his patients sound like victims of his experiments — some were successful, others were not so — but who had been there to stop the doctor from doing anything he wished in order to advance his own knowledge of medicine? Isaac realised the answer was simply no one.

'My leg, though, it is there, isn't it? What of my leg, sir?' Isaac's slurred voice sounded very timid.

'I am afraid that I had to give it a bit of a knock and a tug before re-strapping it. Oh, it should heal well enough with rest. It was already mending, but not in the right place. It had not set right at all in the joint. Perhaps in haste they splinted it but had not time to straighten the joint accurately.' He coughed and then casually added, 'But it is all good now. You must have plenty of bed rest for a week or two and then mobility will be slow. Certainly keep your weight off it completely for three or four days until you can walk with crutches. I would suggest that you allow him to use that old basket chair of your mother's, Sir Kenneth. There will be some muscle wastage and that too will need time to regain strength and movement. But, with good nursing and with no further infection you could be looking at walking without a stick in a month and riding again in three. The key is not to rush at the recovery and undo our good work.' The doctor was smiling.

'Perhaps I could use my old accommodation, sir, until I can move more freely?' Isaac said, and saw the looks of disbelief exchanged by Brent and Robert. They clearly did not think that was a good idea. Isaac had burdened Sir Kenneth with his unexpected arrival and now his slow recovery was at the mercy of the man who he had wronged by falling in love with his daughter.

'Wouldn't hear of it, Dalesman! You can look upon this as your room until you are well enough to walk out of it on your own feet, unheeded by crutches. Then we will talk of what you should do next.' Sir Kenneth patted him on the shoulder. 'You are my house guest and I will make sure we keep a keen eye on you and that your steps do not falter in any way again. Rest easy, my lad, and thank God for your good fortune, and that you have a willing benefactor to steer your future out of what would otherwise have been a desperate and dark one. We wouldn't want that, would we, Dalesman?' The question was rhetorical. 'Take heart and obey my instructions in all things.' His face was still emotionless. 'You should be well practised in taking orders by now.'

Isaac could only feel gratitude to the man, for he had nowhere else to go and was hardly in a position to leave even if he had. He would be watched, that was the undeniable message, but he stood a chance of walking straight again and that was all he cared about. Patience and goodwill were the watchwords he would live by. His other business would have to wait.

'Archibald, thank you, my dear friend. You have done a great service here. Join me for a brandy?' Sir Kenneth said, as he left the room with his friend.

Brent came over to the bedside. 'Isaac, you have risen well in society. Take care not to abuse the master's hospitality. Sorry about your father. Joshua was a good man.' He turned around and walked out.

'Who would have thought that under that ironclad shell Brent actually has a heart?' Isaac said to Robert.

'You do not know him at all. He has a heart that is passionate about his master and defiant against anyone who would wrong him. But he has the jaw of a bull-dog and sharp teeth, so heed his words.' Robert leaned against the end bedpost. 'You jammy sod, Isaac,' he said. 'If you fell over in a pigsty I swear you'd miss all the shit!'

'Robert, God help me, I thought he'd sawed it off. Heaven preserve what dignity I have left, man, but I nearly fell to pieces at the thought,' Isaac blurted out his words with passion, his eyes and face filled with relief.

'You may be a hero in the field, with canons blasting and men screaming and God only knows what other mayhem, but you are still human and allowed to feel fear and pain. Anyway, since when did you worry about 'dignity'? How you have changed!'

Isaac looked up at him almost apologetically, for he had changed — he had had to survive enemies both opposing and inside his own army.

Robert continued, 'Don't doubt it, man, I would have screamed, the knock he gave that leg bone I thought he was trying to split it open again; it was enough to make my toes curl up. The thought of a crack nearly turned my stomach, mind, and I am used to butchering the pigs when needs be. He said it could have worked itself loose and come through the skin if it had been left. Gosh, I'd have hated to see you left on the streets of Gorebeck begging and wasting away . . .' His words drifted off. 'Count your blessings, man. You'll be riding again by the end of the year. Stop your fussing and think about how you intend to woo Miss Sophia Baxter-Lodge with that lecher Lucas Huntley sniffing around.' Robert folded his arms across his chest with a cheeky grin.

'Robert, please. Time and place.'

'I can shave you if you wish and make you all pretty again.' Robert was laughing at Isaac's raised eyebrows.

'Perhaps tomorrow. I have had enough torture for today, thank you. What do you mean about Lucas Huntley?' Isaac was all ears. If the man was aiming his attention at Sophia and he was trapped, immobile in a bed, then she was in danger unless he could warn her. Perhaps he could trust Robert to get a message to her? Or perhaps he could simply trust Sophia's judgement, and her heart?

'Well, I heard Brent tell Mrs Gribbins that word had it Mr Huntley broke off his last engagement. Don't know why but know he did.'

'Why is he a guest of Sir Kenneth's then if he is such a lowlife?' Isaac asked.

'Look, you set your mind about getting better and I will keep an eye on what Mr Huntley gets up to. He would not dare to cross his father's friend, I'm sure.'

'Tell me about Pa? Did he suffer long?' Isaac asked.

Isaac had known Robert since they

were both boys serving in the stables, doing all the hard graft of mucking and sweeping out, grooming, polishing. His father had taught them both well. They could both now break in a horse by whispering in the animal's ears then gently slipping onto its bare back and holding on whilst it gave in to their will. He swallowed. Isaac had missed his father so much when he was sent away.

'No, Isaac, he was right as rain on the morning of the day he died. He was uncharacteristically tired by luncheon and dropped dead on the floor before dinner. No one would have been more surprised than he himself. It was like his heart just stopped.' Robert walked around the bed and patted Isaac's shoulder. 'He didn't suffer.'

'Really? You wouldn't say those words just to smooth over the truth for me?' Isaac asked, for he dearly wanted this to be true — no suffering — no illness — no prolonged degenerate old age — just life one minute and death the next.

Robert shrugged and shook his head.

‘When have I ever been that tactful? No, it is as I said, Isaac — his number was up.’ Robert swallowed, quietly adding, ‘He just left us.’

Isaac nodded. He had no wish to press the matter further. Robert’s eyes were sad and Isaac had forgotten that his father was as an adoptive one to his friend too. Then he remembered the flowers laid across the grave in Gorebeck and felt a swell of regret, grief and guilt mixed, for it was not Isaac, his only son, who had been there when his father had needed him the most. Instead the growing certainty that it was the worry over Isaac’s shameful departure and future as a soldier at war might have caused his untimely death. He would never know for sure, but the guilt weighed Isaac down.

‘When I am mobile please show me where he fell.’ Isaac wanted to say a silent prayer on the very spot and hope and believe his father would hear it and then they could both move on.

Robert nodded.

'Please ask Mrs Gribbins what she can do to ensure that my leg does not turn bad, Robert,' Isaac pleaded. 'I know the doctor may well be a good physician, but she knows how to keep the body strong so it can fix itself.'

'You simple dote, you don't still believe in old Gribbins' remedies? God in heaven, man! Next you'll be asking her to burn herbs and waft 'em under and over your wound!' Robert mimicked an incantation as he flurried his hand in the air above Isaac's prone body.

'Robert, that's wicked to talk like that. Even now it could end badly for her if people started making those kinds of aspersions. Ignorance and superstition can cause grief.'

'Aspersions, is it? Not gossip or tittle-tattle? You have been schooled, my friend. Anyway, do as you are told. The doctor has left medication and clear instructions as to how it is to be used. He uses a brown liquid that is supposed to stop the badness settling in. I know it isn't cheap, so don't you do anything that will prevent it from working. No silly potions, eh? When you see them stitches, that yellowy colour is not you going off, but the ointment stuff, healing it for good. You, it appears, are being looked after special like. Why? I know not, for I thought Sir Kenneth would have had you whipped around the estate if you ever showed that handsome face of yours here again. Still, there's much he don't know, isn't there, Isaac?' Robert winked.

Isaac looked back at him but said nothing as he did not like the underlying insinuation. Friends must always be loyal, like his men had been, or they were not friends at all. Isaac wondered if he were being unjust in his feelings.

Robert continued, 'Being turned out at the moment would be your death knell. You have to stay away from Miss Sophia. You do not see it, Isaac, but she toys with you. She knows that she'll eventually be matched to old money. Don't go there again, Isaac.'

'Thank you, Robert, for your words

of wisdom. I shall heed them all, but I think you misjudge Sophia, and time will show you the truth of it. However, I know that you only speak out of concern and for that I sincerely thank you. Now, I would love to see Mrs Gribbins and, as I cannot slip down to the kitchens right now and surprise her, I wondered if . . .' he let his words drift off as he tilted his head on one side and smiled up at Robert.

'I'll see if I can weave my magic for thee and bring the old dear up to you.'

'Thank you,' Isaac said.

'I've missed you . . . sir.' Robert winked at him and left, leaving Isaac feeling strangely vulnerable and alone.

14

Sophia was about to take the air. She needed to clear her head. Somehow Isaac must mend, whilst they made plans. After waiting so long it seemed unbearably cruel to have him close and still banned from her affections. Her father must come to understand that they were deeply in love. How to touch his heart, though, when it was iron-clad?

Sophia popped into the morning room on her way out. 'Morning, Cynthia, I am just going to go for a stroll — would you care to join me?'

'It is such a lovely day. What an excellent notion. We shall join you.' Cynthia stood up.

'We?' Sophia looked further into the room and saw Mr Lucas Huntley standing by the window. He cut a fine figure in his buckskin breeches and highly polished cavalryman's boots. Ironic really, Sophia thought, as he wore them as a fashion when Isaac had earned his right to the whole uniform. The fitted black tailcoat only served to accentuate his height. Somehow the straight edged simplicity of the embroidered waistcoat toned down the effect of the intricately worked gold thread on the black fabric. He was a man who spent his money on quality garments, that was plain to see.

Staring directly back at her, Lucas showed an appreciative sparkle in his eyes — he seemed to be aware of the impact his appearance had on her.

'How marvellous,' he said and picked up his hat, placing it carefully over his dark wavy hair.

'Splendid,' Cynthia exclaimed. 'Give me two minutes and I shall attire myself appropriately. I shall send that young maid for my cornflower parasol or else my skin will gain the likeness of a tomato and we cannot have that, can we?' She giggled.

'Then you would be the most delicately tempting tomato I have ever seen,'

Lucas quipped and Cynthia beamed at him.

Sophia half-smiled — he had such a smooth tongue, honeyed words. Well practised, she thought. She watched Cynthia walk briskly out. Both she and Mr Huntley stood awkwardly looking across the room at each other.

'She may be a few minutes more than two,' Sophia said and smiled.

'I expect the lady will be, as silk slippers are not suitable for a turn around the garden no matter how light of foot the wearer may be. So, could I dare to suggest that we step outside into the front garden by the ornate sculpture of cupid's fountain where we may be clearly seen, but where we may enjoy the fine weather?' He gestured towards the doorway.

'Very well.' Sophia nodded and then walked outside, feeling the warmth of the sun on her cheeks. The birdsong made her heart sing as she thought of the long summer months to come and the joy of extended daylight hours into the evening — so much to enjoy. The wide brim of her bonnet prevented her from squinting as she glanced up at Mr Huntley.

They stood admiring the water in the fountain as it spouted from the mouths of four fishes all pointing towards the central figure of cupid holding his bow high, when a gust of wind clipped the spray nearest them and they felt the moisture in the air as the breeze wafted the flow of water directly at them. Sophia stepped back, as did Mr Huntley, and the air stilled again so that the water's spray returned to its intended target.

Lucas laughed. 'Perhaps I should have suggested we stayed away from the fountain and walked in the shelter of the walled garden? My apologies, Miss Baxter-Lodge. You see I have always loved art and sculpture and cupid is such a lovely prophetic piece, is he not?'

'You need not apologise. I can hardly expect you to be able to predict what the wind will do at any given minute, Mr Huntley,' she said as they walked around the edge of the fountain together, ignoring his rather odd question.

'Tell me, please, before your chaperone returns, what interests you most in life, Miss Baxter-Lodge?' Lucas asked and Sophia glanced back at him, trying to cover up her surprise by this forthright, and again rather odd, question. 'An honest answer, please, would be greatly appreciated, not a prepared one made ready for possible suitors greeted at the assembly rooms.' He seemed very serious, so Sophia did not offer a quip by way of a reply.

'I hardly think that question would be one I could have prepared for at such a gathering as I have never heard it asked before. It is rather a strange one, sir.'

'Strange or not, please humour me and answer it now,' he said.

'Life,' Sophia answered honestly.

'Life?' he repeated and stopped, somewhat bemused.

'Yes, nature, people, the estate, food, literature, news from my father's visits to town, the welfare of the estate workers . . .' She stopped. He seemed to be absorbing every word she spoke. 'What interests you most?' she returned as Cynthia appeared on the steps of the Hall, ready to join them.

Sophia thought that he would not have time to answer, but then he replied as simply as she had. 'You do,' he whispered, as he stepped forward to greet Cynthia with a gentlemanly nod.

Sophia bit her lip as no answer was needed or expected from her. How slick he was, but Sophia wondered what game he was playing. She stifled a smile. He had a way about him that was charming. His conversation with Cynthia turned to the new rose beds and the Grecian folly Cynthia was planning. Sophia followed on and let their friendly banter wash over her. What a very peculiar man he was, she thought. She had not been completely honest in her answer to him because the one interest that overwhelmed her was Isaac.

They continued to stroll around the Hall's gardens. She glanced up to Isaac's bedchamber and wished that he was there at her side, walking with a confident and even gait like Lucas did. Her thoughts were interrupted by the man who had been keeping a watchful eye upon her without her realising it.

'Forgive me, Miss Baxter-Lodge,' Lucas Huntley said, 'as I forget myself and take your dear mama's attention, leaving you to straggle on behind like the lost sheep.' Lucas was standing squarely in front of her, commanding her full attention.

Sophia stopped abruptly. 'You need not apologise, Mr Huntley, for I can assure you I am rarely lonely when in my own company and I never 'straggle'.'

Cynthia laughed and hooked Sophia's arm in the crook of hers, before her voice could become more confrontational. Sophia had often been informed by her father that that was a quality that did not sit well in a lady of position. 'Come, dear, there is no need for you to be alone today. We shall go and see how your horse fares, Mr Huntley. I heard he was a Thoroughbred — a fine beast,' Cynthia enthused.

'You know your horse flesh, madam?' he asked, looking impressed.

'Indeed, my father used to cross Arabians for their speed with our own local mares for their strength. As a girl I would hear him talk of them at the dinner table, much to my mama's chagrin, but we are a county that loves our horses, are we not, Sophia?'

Sophia decided to play along with their polite banter. 'We certainly do. Father has an ever growing interest in them,' she added but then thought perhaps it made him sound like a gambling man, which as far as she knew he was not. Then again, had he not won Cynthia by gambling with her brother? So perhaps he had more of an interest in racing than she was aware of.

'It is the sport of kings and, therefore, we are being extremely patriotic, are we not, by engaging with it?' Lucas laughed. 'There is no harm in a little flutter; we should all try occasionally — well, not a lady, perhaps.' He winked at Cynthia playfully.

'Indeed so. Tell me, did you go to the Ledger last year?' Cynthia walked them onwards and the general air of the conversation lightened into the banal. Sophia listened to them as they approached the stable.

Robert Judd was just about to leave the building when Lucas asked him how his horse's leg was.

'Well, sir,' Robert Judd answered. His eyes stared directly into Sophia's and not at Mr Huntley's face, challenging to her in a way she did not understand. It was an intense glare, and it unnerved Sophia. She had always been a little shy of the man, suspecting he had been in Isaac's confidence at some point in the past and, if so, she knew that there had been more unpleasant gossip about her and Isaac than her father knew about.

Sophia turned away from Robert Judd's gaze and was further indisposed when she saw Mr Huntley notice the brief reaction. She could tell he was a very astute man. She hoped that she had not coloured or that he had sensed her awkwardness. It was yet something else she would have to be careful of as he must not find out about her and Isaac. He could do both of them a great deal of damage.

'Ladies, if you would prefer to continue your stroll without me I shall catch you up as soon as I have seen Leviathan.' He smiled at Sophia and gestured to Robert Judd that he should return to the stable.

'Come, Sophia, let us leave Mr Huntley to his beast. I have no wish to walk inside the stables.' Cynthia smiled. She had no intention of bespoiling her skirt hem or shoes.

Sophia found herself being steered away by Cynthia.

'He is a fine beast though,' she whispered to Sophia. 'I think the buckskins suited him fine. Can you imagine him in long trousers, dressed for one of his gentleman's clubs in London?' she giggled when Sophia looked at her shocked.

'You never cease to surprise me, Cynthia,' Sophia said.

'I sincerely hope that I never do, dear, for that would make me feel boring in the extreme and years older than I am, and that I have no wish to because I will be soon enough. Besides, it should not only be men that can admire a person of beauty and Huntley is certainly easy on the eye, is he not?'

'And you a married lady! Whatever would Father say?' Sophia pretended to admonish her.

'He will never know, will he?' Cynthia said.

'No, that he won't.' Sophia laughed and glanced back to the stables, avoiding giving an answer. Mr Huntley seemed engrossed in conversation about his horse with Robert Judd. How easily men were distracted; at least, where money or sports were concerned, she thought.

15

Isaac should not have been out of bed but he had sat up, slid down to the end and was contemplating his next move. A foot stool had been left by the window seat so that he could prop his leg on it. Very carefully he lifted himself up by the strength of his arms, holding on tight to the bed post. He put his weight on his good leg, swinging his body as gently as he could and leaned against the wall, sliding down onto the window seat. His damaged leg was painful, but thankfully he had not slipped. Just to be able to see the outdoors, a distant view of sheep grazing in the fields beyond the stable block was like a glimpse of heaven to him.

From here he could look down fondly on his old home. It made Isaac feel connected with the Hall instead of like an imposter trapped inside it. Every day here as he became stronger would be a blessing. He heard voices below and leaned forward, lifting the window slightly. He could make out the familiar tones below. There was the lovely voice of his Sophia, along with Cynthia and Lucas. He craned to watch them, wishing he could run down and join the group. Sophia was beautiful, Cynthia elegant and Lucas — well, he was looking like a peacock, he thought.

When Robert Judd appeared he saw him and Lucas go into the stables. 'Good man, Robert!' Isaac muttered. 'You keep him away from my Sophia.'

'What in blazes do yer think yer doing, Isaac Dalesman?'

The voice caught him off guard. Isaac jumped, nearly unseating himself. His head shot around to see Mrs Gribbins place what smelt like her delicious chicken broth on the bedside table.

'Mrs G!' he said, his face lighting up as he tried to stand.

Rushing to his side she grabbed hold of him under his armpits and swung him back to sit upright on the edge of the bed. Years of kneading bread dough and moving heavy pots and pans around a kitchen had made her strong. Once her hold was released she moved the foot-stool and made him inch up the bed so that he was propped up, with the pillows behind his back, whilst she guided his leg carefully back underneath the coverlets.

He winced but did not receive any sympathy. When safely back where he should have been, Isaac held both arms up wanting to hug her properly. His heart was filled with love for he had missed Mrs G, his surrogate mother, and her tasty cooking, sorely.

Rather than hug him she folded her arms across her bust. 'You bloody idiot, Isaac! What if you had fallen upon it? What then?' She shook her head.

'I didn't, though, did I, Mrs G? Oh God, you are a sight for sore eyes. I've missed you so much . . .' He swallowed.

'Aye and me too.' Mrs Gribbins relented and hugged him. Isaac breathed in her familiar musk, which was a mix of lavender from her home-made perfume, blended with the mouth-watering essence of her baking. He had not felt so safe since he first left the Hall.

She straightened up, sniffed, and rubbed away a tear before bustling about the room to find him the tray. 'You should be shaved; you don't suit them whiskers, they make you old before your time. I'll send Robert up later.' She flipped the tray's legs down and placed it in front of him, then carefully put the bowl of broth and spoon upon it and spread a napkin on his chest.

'Are you going to feed me like a baby or can I do that bit myself?' he asked. 'I thought the whiskers made me look more mature, like a gentleman.'

'Cheeky lad, Isaac, you always was, but there was never any harm in you. You don't become a gentleman because you can grow hair on your face. Stop hiding and let us see your face again.'

'I'll think on it,' he said, knowing he would do as she bid him.

'Oh, Isaac, how I worried for thee and then poor Joshua, he . . .'

Isaac stared at her. 'Tell me honestly, what happened to Father?' he asked. Mrs Gribbins looked at her feet and then put her head up with a forced smile. 'Eat your broth; it'll have gone cold.'

'Tell me the truth, Mrs G. I always know when there is something you shouldn't tell me but wanted to. What really happened to him, please?' He picked up his soup spoon to appease her.

'Very well, but you cannot change a thing and you still need to eat that.' She pointed to the bowl and he nodded and sipped his first spoonful, although his appetite had suddenly left him.

'Well, he was ripe as a peach that morning at breakfast and went about his normal day.'

Isaac felt like sighing as this seemed to be a pre-arranged script, but before he could tell her to stop if she was going to give him the same version of events as Robert, the tone of her voice changed.

'I tell you, he was fine, his normal self, but then that night he took a heavy fall and when he was found in the early hours of the next morning he was just lying there, cold and alone. Oh Isaac! It near broke my heart to see such a fine man go like that. He loved you dear and, well, he'd be so proud of what you have achieved.' Mrs Gribbins wiped away a tear.

'You say he fell in the stables? At night?' Isaac could not believe his ears.

'Yes, he never drank; your father was always dry, so he must have had a fit or dropped dead on the spot. Robert was beside himself when he discovered what happened to him. He cried like a baby for an hour. I thought his heart was going to break too. Then Sir Kenneth said your father would have a proper service in the estate chapel and be buried in Gorebeck behind St Peter's where your ma and pa were wed. It was a place he loved. Sir Kenneth even paid for a headstone and insisted you were named on it too . . .'

Isaac nearly dropped his spoon. He had not expected such a thoughtful gesture from the master of the house, seeing as Sir Kenneth had been the one who had separated them in life. Isaac tried to smile. 'I've seen the grave, Mrs G. I should have been there for my father when he needed me and I should have been the one who paid for it. But I can at least repay that. I made a mess of my father's life.'

'No, lad, you made him proud. But, my God, you mind what you get up to this time. That lass is not 'your Sophia'. I overheard your sentimental ramblings about her, and that means others may too. Them young maids will likely report back to Sir Kenneth. They do not have the loyalty that us older ones do.'

'Where was Robert the night it happened?' Isaac asked.

'He were in Gorebeck. That's why he took it right bad. He said he should have been there to save him. That's fate for you though. None of us can be certain of what lies ahead, can we? Healthy one minute, dead the next. Makes you wonder sometimes what the point of it all is.' She sniffed. 'Sorry, don't mean to blaspheme none. Listen, love, I've got to get back to me puddings or they'll be cinders. You finish that up and I'll send young Maisey for the tray.' She stood up. 'Isaac, your father never did blame you for wanting the lass, or Sir Kenneth for sending you off to war with the horses.'

'Thank you, Mrs G, for telling me the truth,' he said.

'That is the least I can do. Remember, lose the beard and be proud of the man you are.'

'Very well, for you, I will,' he said.

Mrs Gribbins nodded and went back downstairs, leaving Isaac to his thoughts. Isaac shook his head. 'Oh, Pa? What the hell happened to you?' The silence told him he may never know and that pained him greatly.

16

'Where is Father, Cynthia?' Sophia asked. Cynthia was reclining on the chaise longue in the orangery, happily basking in the warmth of the day. A crystal jug of her favourite daytime drink, lemon water, was on the table next to her.

'He has taken Mr Huntley to the races, or the other way around. I'm not sure whose inspiration it was. No matter — they're away and we have some peace. I am not expecting them back before Thursday at the earliest.' She did not open her eyes. 'Two whole days to do nothing . . . What absolute bliss. Unless another hero crosses our path, needing care.'

'Enjoy your peace, Cynthia,' Sophia said and left, going straight up the stairs toward Isaac's bedchamber. She had a book in her hand as she had originally intended to join Cynthia and read a while, expecting Mr Huntley to be hovering near her again, but with both he and her father away, every moment she had free must be used to her advantage — this was her chance to see Isaac alone.

Sophia paused on the upper landing to make sure there were no servants around, and that Robert Judd, who had a habit of slipping in to spend time with Isaac whenever he could, was nowhere to be seen. Entering Isaac's bedchamber through the small bathing room next door as the servants would, she saw Isaac was sitting up in the bed, staring out of the window.

'Whoever you are, please enter and save me from a slow and painful certain death by boredom.' He had not looked around.

'Well, we cannot have that, can we?' Sophia said, watching his head snap round at the sound of her voice. He was staring at her with grateful eyes, ones that betrayed how happy he was to see her.

'Oh, Sophia!' He tried to change position. She ran to his bedside and sat carefully on the edge of the bed, holding his shoulders gently to make him sit back straight. She felt the solid, strong muscle beneath the fabric of the nightshirt and realised how much he had matured since she had hugged that nervous youth of yesteryear. 'You should not be in here,' he said, but with little conviction and a very happy face.

His eyes were moist, his colour slightly high. She could see that he was clearly ailing. He needed this rest.

'Do you have a fever, Isaac?' she asked.

'Not the type that Dr Aimes could cure, but, Sophia, we are undone should anyone see you here, like this, on my bed.' He groaned. 'I have dreamt of you being on — no, in — my bed and here we are, but look at the state I'm in. I will die if I am sent away from here in this condition. My leg has to be saved if I am to be any good to anyone — to you. You should leave . . .' he said with a heavy heart.

'I will stay and read to you awhile. Father is away with Mr Huntley for a few days.'

'If your father should find out . . .' he whispered.

'He won't. I believe that Cynthia is in favour of our friendship, but how much she knows and how, I have no notion. However, she is perfectly happy for me to spend some time with you, of that I am certain.'

'You are beautiful,' he said.

'Oh, Isaac, you have not forgotten me. I was so scared you would be killed or, worse, fall in love with a beautiful woman in some exotic land.'

He sat forward and she saw his eyes widen in amusement. 'Believe me, where I have been there was nothing exotic about it. I was too busy staying alive to look at other young maids.'

'Good, so tell me of some of your brave exploits.' Sophia waited and he looked at her as if he was going to share something, but then he seemed to change his mind so she quickly changed the subject. 'Let me read to you.'

Isaac took her hand. 'I do not aim to offend you by my silence, but I want to leave what happened out there and not taint you or this precious place with it.' He lifted his arm up and stroked her shoulder with his hand. She gently leaned forward and rested her head upon his chest, giving him a tender hug.

'Tell me if I hurt you, Isaac,' Sophia said. A few moments passed by in waves of inner bliss. Here, wrapped in his arms, the emotions inside Sophia were overwhelming, heady and delightful. When finally they parted she knew they had restarted their friendship again exactly at the point where fate had made them part years earlier. Yet she was now a woman full grown and he was a man of the world.

'What are we to do?' she asked. She stood up and folded the sheet back over the top of the coverlet.

'Be patient. We have no choice. We shall, however, find a way for our union to happen . . . officially.'

Sophia glanced at him quickly and then at the door lest anyone was there. She should feel guilt for they had crossed lines in more ways than one, but their desire had been so strong and their commitment total. Still, she blushed.

He shook his head. 'You and I are soulmates; we should be forever joined, always together. How else do we explain the way we know each other so well, despite having nothing in common by birth right? I am no longer an infatuated boy, Sophia. I think there may well be a way for us to marry, but I need to be able to walk straight and seek it out before I can talk again of it with your father. That will take time. Feel no regret at our previous transgressions because I will never forsake you.'

'I would give you as much time as you need, Isaac. But Father has Mr Lucas Huntley in his sights for me, I am sure of it. He wants you to be mended and does not appear to hold a grudge, but he will not bless our marriage ever, and that breaks my heart, for I do not wish to break his.' Sophia leaned forward. 'It appears we face an insurmountable problem, but we will somehow overcome this.' She stared out of the window. 'If Mr Huntley was not so personable it would help, but he ingratiates himself with Father daily.'

'And what of you?' Isaac asked, his voice low and quiet. 'Are you ingratiated?'

'What do you mean?' Sophia smiled at him, flattered by his show of rivalry, but she could plainly see that Isaac had been thinking about Mr Huntley whilst lying in his sick bed, his thoughts turning to jealousy toward the fit and moneyed man who had both her attention and her father's approval. She could not bear to see him suffer anymore and had not the heart to tease him further.

'Those thoughts are unworthy of you, and me, and so is the question. Do not think them anymore.' Sophia saw relief in his strained features.

'Very well, I apologise,' Isaac said. 'You and I will be together, but you must not risk seeing me here again. Servants talk, you know. Wait until I am able to convalesce downstairs, seated in the orangery or the garden. Then, where we may be watched, you can read to me, or entertain me with your enlightening and witty conversation.' Isaac's lips fixed in a determined line. 'I will be allowed out of bed by Sunday, Cynthia promised me.'

'How will we win Father over, Isaac?' Sophia looked beseechingly into his eyes, determined not to acknowledge the obvious doubt of his recovery that threaded through his words. 'What business can you possibly have to discuss with him that would change his view of our situation? You cannot change your birth right any more than I can mine. All I can do is walk away from it, but . . .' She swallowed, lifted her chin, and added, 'I would do that for us.'

Isaac coloured slightly. 'Believe me, the option of being able to walk away should never be dismissed lightly. However, I would never ask you to do that. My business concerns an investment of sorts in horses.'

Sophia raised her eyebrows. Surely he knew too much about the animals than to risk his hard earned pay on gambling on one.

'There is a way, but it will take time and a trip to London,' Isaac continued. 'Until then, you and I will have to be careful and our actions seen to be above reproach. We need your father's trust first and then his love will surely follow,' Isaac said.

'You are annoyingly correct, just as you were back then,' Sophia replied. 'It was my eagerness that brought us low and it will be your strength and honour that will raise us high. I will do as you say, but I am worried that arrangements for a match with Mr Huntley may be underway as we speak. His father was supposed to be here, looking to match my annoying cousin Annabelle to Lucas, but somehow things do not seem so straightforward now. Lucas has turned up in the old man's stead and seems to be charming Father. Have we the time to make our blessed union happen, Isaac?' She swallowed, reading his expression of concern.

'You must slow things down — interfere with their plans,' Isaac told her. 'Once Huntley has set off to London to report to his old man then time will be our own again. I do not know this man well. But he has secrets, Sophia. Tell me what you have learned of him?' Isaac inched himself up the bed a little so he was more upright. His forehead creased with pain as he flinched at the effort.

Sophia explained about the business that the Huntleys would be setting up in Australia. When she saw the change in Isaac's face she stopped talking.

'What is it?' Sophia asked. 'Have you heard of the father, Mr Charles Huntley?'

'No, but I have been slow in the extreme. I knew Lucas Huntley had intentions to travel to Australia but not that he was actively seeking a wife to take with him. He clearly seeks more from this deal with your father than to buy sheep. Can you fetch me a pen and paper quickly, and please be discreet? I need you to act as my accomplice in this matter, but act with haste we must. I have already sent letters from Gorebeck on my way here, but now that things have moved on apace I must chase matters up as I cannot return to the London offices as soon as I had intended to.'

'To see who, Isaac?' Sophia was perplexed — he was speaking in riddles.

'My representatives in the City. Until I have a reply to my letter no one must know that I have sent it. I should have travelled down in person, before now. They may well wonder why I have not returned again in person. Trust me, for I do not wish to be questioned upon it.' Isaac was holding her hand tightly.

'Why? What is the urgency?' Sophia asked.

'It is as I said. Please just trust me on this, Sophia.' Isaac's words were abrupt.

To Sophia it was as if he were giving an order in the army — 'Obey me!' She pursed her lips and glared back at him.

'Do not treat me like a child.'

'Do you not see, Sophia? If this man's fortune and future lies in Australia then any wife he takes will be at his side. I would lose you forever . . .'

'You would lose me forever, Isaac, if I married *any* other man!' she said, but he ignored her outburst and continued calmly.

'I know that! The thought of another man having you has dogged me night and day for years. Lucas Huntley's and your father's plans may be hurried along to fit in with his sailing date. God, how I bristle with frustration!' He clenched his fists. 'You cannot be another man's wife, Sophia — you will be my wife,' he added quietly.

A tear escaped Sophia's eyes as she saw the distress this revelation caused in him. To leave England, leave Isaac so soon, when he had just found her again and to abandon her father forever was almost too much for her to bear. Even the thought of never hearing Cynthia's girlish and impish laugh made her want to sob. Yet Cynthia had encouraged her to consider Lucas, hadn't she? Did this mean she wanted Sir Kenneth all to herself?

Sophia wanted to create a family home that embellished her own, Fenton Hall. Cynthia would be adorable as a grandmamma. She swallowed again because she thought of her own mother dying in childbirth and taking her brother with her, which made her fear for her own future even more. But there was something else burdening her deep in her soul which was more troubling still. It was the way Isaac spoke of her being HIS wife. Did she always have to belong to someone? Could she never be her own person?

'Maisey, check that the lieutenant is comfortable,' Brent's voice resounded down the landing outside the bedchamber.

Sophia ran towards the other room without further words being spoken, but her mind was filled with so many unanswered questions. She would return later with quill, ink and paper and his letter would be written. Had her father already sanctioned this match with Lucas Huntley? Would he really want to send her so far away? Was Cynthia sufficient family for him to live contentedly with in England alone? Surely not!

'Go, quickly, Sophia . . .' The whisper drifted on the air as she closed the door.

She nodded, her reverie broken, and left.

17

Isaac could not sleep. The night hours dragged out before him. He tried counting sheep, his blessings, the minutes . . . seconds . . . but nothing helped. Something had happened when Sophia had last spoken to him, which was unsettling. He had called her his and she had frozen and not fallen into his arms. But who could blame her? How could he look after her as a man should when he could not even leave his bed without the aid of Robert Judd to support him? He would ask Sophia if she was having doubts, if she wanted to wait and see what happened. But the threat of Lucas whisking her off to the other side of the planet was not to be borne.

He felt a waft of stale cold air on his cheeks and knew that he was no longer alone. A slim frame sat next to him on the bed. His senses awoke. Perhaps he had read Sophia's reaction wrong? It seemed she had returned to him.

'Tell me you are not a spectre, or my disrespectful past come to haunt me?' Isaac whispered in her direction.

Sophia did not say a word but she leaned forward over him, gently so as not to disturb his leg. Oh, how his body ached for her, more than the wound that throbbed and itched in turn. Normally so active, to him this was like purgatory, a penance to behold for his sinful thoughts and desires.

'It is late,' he said. 'You had better light a lamp.'

She had carried her writing box in as he had requested. He held the paper up to her and then set to dictating a letter of apology to his agents in London for not having been there in person. He continued to ask for a confirmation, by return, the monies now available to him and that his previous orders and purchase had been fulfilled.

Sophia finished writing and looked at him. 'Are you going to expand further upon this to me?' she asked him.

‘When I have my reply all shall be clear and our world can open up to us.’

* * *

Sophia collected her things and slipped into the servants’ room, but she nearly dropped the writing box when she bumped into the solid figure of Mrs Gribbins who had just entered from the other door.

‘You scared me!’ Sophia said defensively as she clutched the writing box in front of her, the letter carefully concealed within.

Mrs Gribbins held the candle in her hand and lifted the holder slowly up and down as she took in the sight of Sophia in her nightdress and bare feet. ‘Well, miss, you are traipsing around like a spirit of the night.’ Mrs Gribbins stared at her; disapproval dripped off her tongue.

Sophia tried to sound dignified and held her head up high. ‘I needed my writing box,’ she said, and went to step past Mrs Gribbins, but the woman blocked her way.

'Well, I hope you got what you wanted, miss, because that man in there is a real hero and deserves better! His life depends on your father's beneficial nature. One wrong step, if you'll pardon the pun, and he will be out on his . . . Well, he wouldn't be standing, that's for sure. So if you've finished your night walking, may I suggest that you return to your own room and have Judd fetch anything you need from Isaac's bedchamber in future?'

Sophia took a step backwards. 'How dare you speak to me in that manner!' Sophia snapped, but she kept her voice low as she had no wish for anyone else, including Isaac, to know of this unfortunate meeting.

Mrs Gribbins came so close that Sophia was scared the candle may set her hair alight. 'How dare *I* ? Does your father or Lady Baxter-Lodge know where you are? Dressed in your bedclothes! Coming out of Isaac's room? Have a care, girl. His life is in your hands.'

'You go too far!' Sophia said.

Mrs Gribbins stepped up close to her. 'No, lass, I do not. *You* do, and you damned well know it! But I will not tell on you, for it would be my Isaac who would take the fall again, and you shall not report me for the same reason. So just this once, miss, you take my advice — forget that I am a lifelong servant in this household, and look on it as advice from a friend — and I am one, for I know you two are right together. Now get yourself off to bed before we are both undone, and do not think that young man will get through this night without a sound talking to from me either. Even when a man lays ill abed he still thinks through his . . . and not his head. God help womenfolk from the stupidity of lust and love. And God save a man who is trapped abed by the whims of a foolish maid.'

Sophia ran out of the door and down the hallway to her own room. Never had she felt so ashamed in her life. Had Mrs Gribbins known of their previous trysts? She breathed deeply to return her calm.

If she was to do anything in the Hall she must remember that it was not just her father, Lucas or Cynthia who she had to watch — the household staff had eyes everywhere. Beyond her all-consuming embarrassment, though, she had enough sense to be able to determine a friend from a foe and knew Mrs Gribbins would never betray her Isaac.

18

Sophia had not visited Isaac for two days but Robert Judd still burst into his room daily. Isaac laughed as the man bowed in a grandiose fashion after he entered, outdoing any dandy in London.

'Get up, man, before you start grovelling on the floor like an ant.'

'What a fine queen you would make, Isaac!' Robert closed the door and produced a small flask from his coat pocket. 'Your humble worker-bee has brought you some much needed nectar.' He offered it to Isaac, after removing the stopper.

Isaac took a welcome swig and his eyebrows rose. 'Best French brandy, if I am not mistaken.'

Robert retrieved the flask and winked at him. 'Could be Irish, and equally deliciously, heathen,' he replied and chuckled. 'Friend of a friend,' he said and then quickly changed the subject.

'So milad, you are to wash and dress and become familiar with a basket chair. You will be gradually starting your journey to recovery and to riding a horse again. But first things first, let us get you out of that bed, shaved and dressed.' He cheerfully flipped back the quilted coverlet.

'Shaved!' Isaac protested.

'Yes, milad, for milady, Gribbins insists.'

Isaac groaned. 'What news do you bring, Robert? How is Sophia?' Isaac swung his legs together over the side of the bed.

'Well, Mr Huntley is trying very hard to persuade Sir Kenneth that he is ambitious, knowledgeable of horses and fortunate with the nags. He aspires to be interested in breeding from Sir Kenneth's sheep in Australia to impress him. I must say that of the banter between them when they've been out hunting and around the stables they seem to be getting along splendidly — I'm sorry to say. But Mr Huntley does not know the nags like he thinks he does. He is going to bet on a chestnut sold at a recent auction when the money will be made on the grey horse sold beside it.' Robert cleared his throat. 'And as far as I know Miss Baxter-Lodge is well.'

'You duped him!' Isaac realised why Robert had spoken loudly about the chestnut horse at the market. It was so that Lucas would overhear him. So Robert was not so stupid after all.

'You heard that?' Robert chuckled. 'I merely helped out a friend to earn some readies.'

'Did Sir Kenneth and Lucas Huntley mention Sophia at all?' Isaac asked.

Robert whipped off Isaac's nightshirt and then unceremoniously dropped a shirt over his head. 'You've collected a few scars along the way, Isaac. Still, I'm sure Miss Sophia will be impressed when you tell her how you came by them. Women like that sort of hero stuff.' Robert tugged the shirt down firmly. 'Remember not to let that sweet name slip out from your lips, Isaac.'

'Robert, have you heard . . .'

'No, they do not talk of her — well, not whilst I am around, but Mr Huntley watches her a lot.'

'How do you know? Has she been out riding with him?' Isaac glanced at the window for he had only seen her venture out on her own horse.

'Oh, I am trusted by the maids and I know what goes on in this house. If Brent were not so adamant that he will not dress an ex-stable hand himself, I would not be given the pleasure of coming and seeing to you like I do. But it's seen as an honour and raises me up, you see.' He laughed. 'Soon I'll be worthy of licking them boots of yours.'

'Robert, you are my friend and always will be,' Isaac said.

'Aye, but we have to keep up appearances, don't we? Brent sees it as an opportunity for me to practise on you for tending a real gentleman. Then I will be able to help out when they have guests and he is in need of another man's man. You are my mannequin, to dress, and he hopes you know enough, having been in the army, to guide me in some of the skills involved.' He pulled up Isaac's breeches over the injured leg and Isaac winced as Robert was clearly more used to tending the horses than dressing a gentleman, especially one with a sore leg.

'Like I say, Mr Huntley watches Miss Sophia,' Robert continued. 'Maisey said that she thinks he is well drawn to Miss Sophia and that he seeks to woo Sir Kenneth with talk of business and horses before moving onto his real reason for being here. He does not miss an opportunity to have a quiet word with the young miss, or even chance a slight touch of her hand as they walk into dinner. Of course the young miss moves hers away in return. Of course, he has no knowledge that the young 'miss' he is chasing has given her heart away already.'

'Robert, watch him.'

'I already do, for I keep a weather eye on any man who comes into this house. He has a plan, of that I am sure. Mr Huntley is a man who plays his hand close to his chest, but a player he definitely is. It does not mean he is a good player, but at the moment Sir Kenneth is treating him like a long lost friend. I think the old man has been duped.' Robert fetched Isaac's waistcoat and placed it next to him on the bed.

'How has Sophia coped with all this unwanted attention?' Isaac asked, and was not comforted when Robert laughed and sat back on his haunches on the floor as Isaac slipped his waistcoat on.

'She appears to be politely flattered by it, which of course only gives Mr Huntley the idea that he is in with a chance, or that he is home and dry. Why would she not be? Here she is wasting away in this place and then two rivals for her attention arrive at once. Isaac, her life has just become full of possibilities. I fear Miss Sophia is a natural flirt.'

'Robert, do not speculate further about Sophia's character. We love each other and that is the end of it.' Isaac looked sternly at Robert who merely grinned back and shrugged.

'Do not forget, Isaac, it was good old Robert who risked all by covering for you two in the beginning. You cannot trust her, Isaac, you take my advice. Believe me, I know how fickle the female heart is.' His eyes hardened.

Isaac shook his head at Robert. 'You are wrong, man, and they are not all cut from the same cloth.'

'And you are a soldier; so tell me, are they all that gentlemanly in the officer's mess?'

Isaac did not answer but he had a very troubled heart. He knew Sophia loved him, but if this cad was winning over Sir Kenneth then might he also win Sophia over in time?

'When does Lucas Huntley leave, Robert?' Isaac asked. 'Is that horse of his mended yet?'

'It could do with a few more days. He'll leave when he's achieved what he set out to, I suppose,' Robert responded, as he helped Isaac stand upright.

'Then let us disrupt his progress, Robert. We must find a way.'

'I could sabotage the animal further, but I would not stoop so low to hurt an innocent animal. What do you suggest?'

'Get me down the stairs so I can watch him for myself. Meanwhile, be diligent and see if you can find out if he is betting on the horses and, if so, how heavily. Does your cousin still work as a bookie on the tracks?'

Robert nodded.

'Then have a word and find out what Lucas Huntley and Sir Kenneth have been betting on.'

'If I can find him. He gets around, you know. It goes with the job.' Robert stood up and looked down at his friend.

'Has he not stopped by recently?' Isaac asked. 'He used to.'

Robert shook his head. 'You cannot expect everything to have carried on as it did before you went away. I see him occasionally in Gorebeck, so I will see what I can find out. But if Mr Huntley gambles he may well be able to afford the losses. Gentlemen live their lives in debt — it is us paupers who get thrown in clink for it. Sir Kenneth is not one to risk all. So I shall humour you, but I fear you're flogging a dead horse with this one.'

'Thanks, I owe you,' Isaac said.

'Yes, you do — an awful lot.'

19

Isaac had taken to watching the estate by moonlight from the window seat when he could not sleep. He had been given strict instructions from Dr Aimes to try not to twist and turn in the night, so as to encourage his leg to heal straight. Some nights, like tonight, sleep would not come and so he perched on the window seat and watched the stars. The sky was so clear and the moon so bright that the shadows played tricks with his mind. He could see shapes moving, blending, forming . . . or were they real? He could not tell. Perhaps the sheep changed form like werewolves in the night, he mused. He yawned and reluctantly returned to bed. Tomorrow he was determined to stand, propped by crutches, and without the blasted basket chair.

A week had passed by slowly since he had last seen Sophia. He had reluctantly insisted she did not risk coming to him, but he had managed to sit in the conservatory, and so had observed her in the presence of Cynthia, Lucas or her father. She had been allowed to read to him and they talked about the world he had seen, but not the battles he had fought in. They were locked down deep in his soul and were not for the delicate ears of his Sophia.

The night hours dragged on and Isaac only survived the tedium and loneliness by visualising Sophia. Lost and trapped in his thoughts, he returned to lying on the bed waiting for sleep, but a sense of despair was growing within him. How much had Sir Kenneth and Lucas Huntley already agreed about Sophia's future whilst he was discounted as a suitor?

A waft of air drifted over him as the bedchamber's door opened and the essence of Sophia's perfume filled his senses. He felt alive again and was filled with hope for their future, for they belonged together. How bold, he thought, not even coming in via the servants' door. She should not be there, but the desire to feel her presence next to him was almost more than he could bear. His eyes moistened and he had to cough the emotions away. What a romantic he was becoming!

'You must leave me alone, Sophia. I will be walking down the stairs tomorrow, not carried like a baby in that blasted basket chair again.' He squinted through the dark to make out her graceful form as she crossed the room. Her body leaned slightly into his bed and he felt her breath against his cheek, her hand placed carefully next to his. There was only the thickness of his night shirt and her fine evening dress between their bodies.

She did not speak, which raised his anticipation of what she was going to do next. She was being either very brave or very foolish in coming to him on her own under the cover of darkness. He knew Lucas Huntley and Sir Kenneth had left the Hall again to attend an appointment in York.

'Whatever your father and Mr Huntley are playing at it certainly is all engrossing. They have hardly been apart since our arrival,' he whispered.

Sophia was behaving strangely and he could not understand why. He was seriously concerned about what those two men were planning but she was still not saying anything. Something was not right. He felt a curl of her hair touch his cheek and he knew instantly something was very wrong. The faint perfume he had thought he knew so well was no more than the delicate smell of orange blossom. He grabbed the hand. 'Who are you?'

The chuckle was unmistakable, although it was subdued. Cynthia stood back and wrapped her shawl around her, which had slipped off her shoulders as she had approached him. Isaac felt for the table at the side of his bed and was about to try and pull himself upright when she slapped his hand, whilst still standing at his bedside.

'Save yourself the strain. Please forgive me my little test, Lieutenant,' Cynthia whispered and put his hand back by his side. 'Do not distress yourself so. I merely wanted to know if Sophia behaved improperly with you and if you would, given the opportunity, betray her and use her ill.' She laughed. 'It would appear that my suspicions were correct, you two are more experienced lovers than I had hoped. You cover it well when you are up, and show disinterest and restraint at least. I do not think that Mr Huntley has any inkling that you and Sophia have your secret trysts — and nor should he. Kenneth would be livid!'

'You play dangerous games, my lady,' he admonished, then dared to add, 'Are you not ashamed to stoop so low? What gives you the right to behave in such a manner?'

She lit the taper in the low burning fire and ignited the flame in the lamp, then placed it carefully down on his bedside table. Her silhouette was blurred to him as disturbingly was her presence, for he had no interest in flirting with a bored wife, if that was her game.

'Dear Isaac, I had no intention of going

any further — do not flatter yourself on that count. I merely wanted to know if the soldier had honour in his soul, or was baser than an animal. You see, I am a married woman and understand these things; Sophia does not. Be pleased, as you just passed my little test. But I know you will not divulge my direct approach to your love, or my Kenneth, as it would not be in either of our interests. But you have to up your game, young Isaac. Kenneth is increasingly impressed by Mr Huntley. Time is ticking by so unless you want our lovely Sophia to say good-bye to her home and country for good, you will have to act swiftly. Oh, and do not challenge me on my actions, for I do what I like, sir. This is my home and she is my stepdaughter . . . and friend.'

'You say this, ma'am, but how am I to act when I have not been allowed to get out of that infernal old woman's basket chair?' Isaac could feel his cheeks burning with anger and frustration. 'Meanwhile your husband and Lucas Huntley ride to the races and God knows where, arranging who knows what, with my Sophia as a bargaining chip.' This woman had toyed with him like he was her puppet. How dare she test him when he was already brought so low?

'Dear boy, calm yourself, tomorrow I am going to town to collect my dresses for the coming season and will be taking with me the two upper housemaids. Brent has to go to meet his master in town and that will leave Sophia in charge of the house, and you. She yearns for you, Lieutenant. Be daring, be bold . . .' She looked along his body as he lay abed.

'Madam, I do not need instruction on what I would ask a young maid to do . . . or not do, but that would hardly gain me favour with Sir Kenneth, would it? Besides, as you have already established, I am a gentleman!'

She laughed coyly. 'Lucas Huntley has a way of making her laugh, that brings a sparkle to those sapphire eyes of hers, but I see a wolf man and not a sheep. You need to up your game as well.'

'You are shameless!' he shook his head.

'Her heart is mine. I do not need to play such games with her, but Sir Kenneth could arrange her match and that I am unable to influence until I can be up and hold a conversation with him.'

'I am practical and direct,' Cynthia told him. 'She loves you, but Lucas Huntley is a dangerous man. You have to claim your woman, unless you want her torn between affection for her father and love for you!'

'You are incorrigible! She is a lady and I am a . . .'

'You are a hero! You were in her eyes when you were younger and you must be one again. Take charge; show her you are a man, her man! Now, I have noticed that you have received communication from London.'

'How would you know about that?'

'My dear boy, you would be surprised by what I know. It pays to be observant and yet unobserved. Now, tell me what it is you are up to and I promise that I will help you.' She folded her arms and the light of a flickering flame cast a shadow on her face that showed her intensity and determination to have things her way.

'Why?' asked Isaac, his head full of suspicions. 'Why would you go against your husband's wishes and help us?' He inched himself up as he studied her.

'Oh, Lieutenant, I never go against my husband's wishes, but I have to understand what it is you are planning so that I can help to bend his wishes to match ours. You see, I have no wish to see Sophia leave this Hall, let alone the country, and there is plenty of room on this estate for you two to have a happy home here with us. But I will know the truth of your intentions, or you will be sent away, far away. I love Sophia as a baby sister, but I will not have my bliss here ruined by anyone.'

* * *

Sophia slipped back into her bedchamber, silently, even though her legs were shaking and her heart racing. She had spent an hour making herself as sensual as she dared, even wearing her new nightgown. Having bathed and perfumed herself in the eau de toilette of the citrus fruits borrowed from Cynthia, Sophia had washed and dried her hair, letting it cascade freely around her shoulders. With her finely woven silk shawl draped around her shoulders she had tiptoed along the upper corridor to slip into her lover's bedchamber. And when she was presented with the image of Cynthia entering into his bedchamber it had shocked her.

At first, guilt had flowed through her veins as she realised that, had she been moments earlier, it would have been Cynthia who discovered her in there with Isaac. Then guilt was swept away by indignation. Cynthia had, like herself, only a shawl around her fine evening dress. Isaac had not called out for someone! He was not in pain, or needing a servant, for there had been no bell rung or shout made, so what was Cynthia about?

Sophia had intended to follow her and

listen, but try as she might she could not overhear what was going on within. If she burst in to find out what Cynthia's game was then there could be a scene and the whole house would know what had happened. Isaac would be injured further, the revelation about Cynthia's behaviour would break her father's heart and Sophia would be forever imprisoned in the Hall as his keeper. This moment of folly on Cynthia's part would ruin everything for them all. What on earth was the woman thinking?

Sophia decided she would wait in the shadows and when her stepmother reappeared she would make her explain her actions. Why was Isaac not protesting — not sending Cynthia away?

Sophia waited but Cynthia did not reappear, and she grew cold. She determined that she would face them both on the morrow. If they kept this secret to themselves and denied what had happened, then she would disown them both. Mr Huntley could take her to Australia, because her heart would be forever broken.

Sophia went to her bed and stared into blackness, for sleep would not come.

20

Isaac half hopped on his good leg over to his window seat and sat upon it, raising his leg along its length. Isaac stared out of the window, trying to calm down as he had to face Cynthia in the morning as if nothing had happened. He hated games that played with people as if they were pawns. The night sky had a splattering of cloud cover which made the shadows darker, like his mood. Resting his back against the wall, he peered out. Counting sheep would not work tonight, even if he were able to see any of them. He distracted himself from his angry thoughts by thinking of what he would do as soon as he was fully mobile. He must have the proof from London of his business affairs to present to Sir Kenneth with his plan for the stables and the horses. He needed a banker's draft.

His attention was caught by something moving outside. The old chapel that stood on the crest of a small hillock was barely silhouetted, but beyond the outline of the stable block roof something larger than a sheep was in his eyeline. A light flickered within the church. It was an odd hour for anyone to be there, unless the priest could not sleep either. Perhaps it was just his tired mind playing tricks. He peered out again, waiting to see if it reoccurred and he was sure he saw a shape cross the field towards the stable block.

Isaac wished he could dash down the servants' stairs and out by the side of the kitchens, pistol in hand, to see what it was. He did not believe in hobgoblins, or ghosts, so if something was there it was either man or beast. But beasts did not light lamps. He must alert Robert Judd, without bringing panic to the women. Isaac looked at the window frame. If he could not get down there himself he would raise the alarm.

However, as he rose to his feet, balancing so that he could grab the sill and then open it wide, he saw Robert Judd leave the stable and skirt around the side of the building, out of his sight.

'What the hell is he up to?' Isaac muttered.

There was no alarm sounded so whoever it was, they were definitely known to Robert. The thought made Isaac feel ill at ease. Robert's brandy was from a 'friend of a friend' he had said, Isaac thought. Good God! Was he taking in deliveries from the tub men as goods were landed over Ebton way? Did Mrs Gribbins know? Or Sir Kenneth even? Isaac would speak with Robert later. The bloody fool! Once you were linked to smugglers and contraband you could not simply walk away from them. You were tainted by association.

Isaac had a really bad feeling about this, but as the silence of the night had not been disturbed he too stayed quiet. He had more unanswered questions in his head. All the peace of his night had gone. Isaac would not sleep that night as frustration at his immobility and his concern over his friend's nightly ventures filled him with new dread.

* * *

When day broke, Lucas Huntley made his way to the stables. He and Sir Kenneth had returned in the early hours after stopping to drink at the inn in Gorebeck. Sir Kenneth was a strange type, all genteel, yet interested in his horseflesh, could hold his drink and knew also how to have a good time.

Lucas had won well, and he was keen to thank Robert Judd and see if he had any handier tips. Sir Kenneth was like any other man, he liked a winner and Lucas had shown himself to be one.

Lucas liked to be up early and get on with the day. Leviathan seemed to be healing well. He wanted to take the horse with him to Australia and breed from him, but for that he needed him to be strong and healthy.

Looking around the stable, there was no sign of Robert Judd. He walked to the end of the stalls and stared up at the steps that led to the man's quarters. 'Judd?' he called out. There was no answer. Strange, Lucas thought. He had expected him to be up and about early.

Lucas glanced around the well-kept building. The stalls were well tended and kept quite clean. Eight horses seemed content in their stalls and fresh hay lined the floor. One was empty, yet still had hay spread on the floor. Perhaps Robert Judd was out already, Lucas wondered. Curious by nature, he slowly ascended the steps, keeping a keen ear for the noise of a returning man.

Peering over the top steps into the roof space that was Robert Judd's room, he saw the man rolled in a blanket. His booted foot stuck out from over the end. Then he heard a sound from the floor the other side of the man's cot as someone else stirred.

Going back down, Lucas presumed that the man had company for the night, perhaps one of the maids, but to make a wench sleep on the wooden floor was hardly gentlemanly, he mused, but then Robert Judd was no gentleman and the wench, whoever she was, would definitely not be a lady.

Lucas's foot touched the ground as a man's voice was heard above. 'Robert, you fell asleep, we both did. I've gotta get back before I'm missed or I'll be out of a job, and then how do I explain how I pay me rent? C'mon, man, get up and give me a ride to town or I'll be scuppered.'

'Give us a minute, Zach,' Robert Judd said and Lucas heard the two men start to move.

Lucas slowly backed away to the door and returned to the house. So who would have guessed that the strapping, dark-haired, handsome Judd was a Molly? Lucas decided that he must pay more attention to him in future. Was that why Robert Judd kept a watchful eye on him? Lucas smiled. Well he would get a sharp shock if he thought that Lucas leaned that way too. Who would have thought it? Robert Judd would break many a maid's heart as he was a decent looking chap.

Glancing over the stables from the side of the Hall, Lucas saw Robert ride out with a man at his back and head straight across the fields in the direction of Gorebeck. Lucas smiled. He did not care personally what the man's tastes were, but such secret knowledge was as good as gold in his hand and could be used to his advantage. It takes time to gain trust and loyalty and get someone to disclose information, but that time he did not have, so now he would use simple coercion — excellent!

* * *

Isaac was incensed with Cynthia's foolish games. She may be quick of wit but she behaved like a spoilt child. It would be bad enough if Sophia and he were found together, but if Cynthia was, then the whole family would crumble!

Vexed that he had not immediately realised it was not Sophia, and so had given away their clandestine moments to her brazen step-mother, Isaac pulled himself upright and rested upon his crutch. Day was breaking. He saw Robert Judd ride out with another man, heading for town. What emergency had befallen now?

He'd ask Robert what the drama was all about when he saw him next, as well as about the movements he had seen last night. It was time to hobble his way down and surprise everyone by being first to breakfast.

Isaac pulled on his shirt and breeches and rested for a moment on the bed whilst he tried to pull on a boot. Frustrated and defeated, he flopped back. How tired he suddenly felt. He closed his eyes — he was supposed to be dressing, such a simple thing, and yet it was easier to drift back into much needed sleep.

21

If Sophia had been a man, she thought, she would be able to ride away and leave the Hall and all of her problems behind her, but she was not and that irked her more now than at any other frustrating time in her life.

After a fitful sleep she arose early, washed and dressed. The blue sky and bright sunshine outside seemed to mock her dismal mood. She would not be broken. To leave this place, her father and the servants whom she had known most of her life, was a wrench she could hardly comprehend. The place was a tamed wilderness — the villages and the fairs were all a part of the life she knew and loved. Could she really venture abroad and find such happiness elsewhere?

Thinking of Cynthia making such an improper visit to her Isaac lit such a burning anger within her that she stormed out of the room and down to break her fast early.

'Sophia, you are up with the birds.' Her father's voice startled her.

'You are back, Father?' she said and realised that if she showed shock it may be interpreted as guilt of some kind. So she smiled and said happily, 'I am so glad. You are away with Mr Huntley so much that we have missed your presence.'

'Really? I will not be taken in so, for I am sure it is the charms and flattery of Lucas Huntley that you have missed, my dear.' He chuckled and took the book that he had found in the library back into the sanctum of his study.

Sophia balled her fists in frustration, for that was the opposite of what she had meant. She stormed into the morning room where the breakfast table was ready laid.

'Maisey,' she said as the young maid brought in coddled eggs, 'when did Father return? Has Mr Huntley eaten yet?'

'Before light dawned Mr Brent said, and yes, miss, he has,' Maisey answered, before dipping a quick bob and leaving.

Sophia was surprised to learn that her father and Mr Huntley had returned in the early hours — how near to disaster had Cynthia brought them? She shook her head, and yet it was her who he distrusted and not his fickle wife!

Her appetite was poor and so a small roll and a pot of hot chocolate was all she needed to settle her hunger. It did not take her long to finish; she stood and made at a pace for the door to leave when she came face to face with Cynthia entering. She too had risen earlier than her normal habit. Sophia wondered if she had also had a surprise when the men returned so unexpectedly.

Sophia and Cynthia normally shared a pleasant chat before beginning their day together. Today, Sophia had hoped to miss her stepmother entirely and be able to speak to Isaac first. How could the woman behave so brazenly as to slip into a man's bedchamber when her own husband was away on business? How was Cynthia going to face him, and how could Sophia keep up a façade of geniality when so much was happening behind closed doors? She would have to, though. But why had Cynthia picked on Isaac? Someone who was supposedly in love with her step-daughter! Why had she not set her sights on the fitter and richer Mr Huntley? Or was that precisely why she had not? Mr Huntley was too dangerous and able, whereas Isaac was detained under her roof only by the goodwill of her husband. He was therefore indebted to them both. Sophia wondered if Cynthia found her father a total bore. Perhaps she satisfied him, but her stepmother needed more…

'Morning, Sophia, isn't the sun beautiful this morning?' Cynthia said. 'We should go for a walk around the gardens today.' She stopped talking and looked at the table where Sophia's plate was already being cleared away, and then she glanced back at Sophia.

'Yes, it is. So I thought I might go for a morning ride,' Sophia said, knowing that Cynthia hated the notion of riding at any time of the day. She could just about abide carriage rides and the occasional short trip on a gig, but she did not trust her life to the whim of a horse. Besides, the elements did unruly things to her hair, which she simply could not abide.

'Well, you take care and enjoy yourself, but no reckless jumping over things. My uncle died falling off a horse . . . It is not safe or ladylike. You can never be sure what awaits you at the other side of a fence or ditch. Besides, I thought you would be spending time with the young lieutenant today. Your father will return this evening.'

'Do you not know, Cynthia? Father has returned already. Did he not disturb you in the night?' Sophia asked, and saw the shock register momentarily in Cynthia's eyes before she cloaked her emotions behind a set smile.

'Your father is a thoughtful man, my dear, he will have not wanted to disturb me,' she said.

'How thoughtful! Isaac will mend more quickly if he rests undisturbed,

I am certain of it — that is, if he is left in peace to do so.' Sophia responded quickly and walked to the doorway, making no apology for her manner. 'Enjoy your breakfast.' Sophia made to step past Cynthia.

'Sophia!' Cynthia snapped out her name with a sharp edge to her normally friendly voice.

'Yes, Cynthia?' Sophia stopped and stared back. 'Was there something you wanted to say to me?'

'Yes. You are not wearing a riding outfit, my dear,' Cynthia said. Her lips smiled, but her eyes did not.

'I was just going to go up to my room to change. I had only just decided to go for a ride. Was that all?'

'Yes, but be sure you do not fall. We do not want two injured souls lying ill abed with damaged limbs. That would be most inconvenient.'

Sophia did not respond.

'I shall be going to town today,' Cynthia added. 'Is there anything you need, or would like bringing back?'

'No, nothing.' Sophia ran up the stairs and flew into her room to quickly change into her riding outfit.

* * *

Once she returned from her ride, Sophia made sure her father, Cynthia and Mr Huntley were all occupied before she entered Isaac's room.

'Ah, you are a joyful sight for my sad eyes. Did you enjoy your ride?' Isaac asked, adding, 'You must have gone out very early. I dearly wish that I could have gone with you,' he added.

Sophia did not reply. She drew back the heavy curtains and light flooded in. She then opened two of the windows slightly and a warm breeze of air rushed into the stuffy room.

'You are just like that welcome breath of fresh air, Sophia. They are so worried that I will catch a chill that they try and suffocate me in darkness. But Robert Judd will be here within the hour to help me dress, so you should not be here.' He paused, but then added, 'You look quite serious. I merely remind you that we must take care not to be seen to be too familiar in each other's company.'

'No, that would never do . . .' Sophia's voice sounded cold even to her own ears, her words left hanging on the air between them.

Isaac stared at her in disbelief. 'What is wrong, Sophia? Has your father returned early with unwanted news? Are you to wed the Huntley man already? Has an arrangement or announcement been made?' He leaned forward. 'Oh God, I dreaded this news!'

Sophia could see the look of panic spreading across his face. It was almost tempting to draw his agony out further and imply that he had guessed correctly, but whatever had happened the previous night, he was a man who had suffered much already and she was not so cruel. 'No, he has changed his plans and has not gone to the races today with Lucas Huntley. There is no such news,' she said in her normal voice, but her heart felt sad. Looking at Isaac, how could she believe he would betray her — betray their love?

Isaac glanced anxiously at the door. 'Then you cannot stay,' he said, but was obviously surprised when she did not move.

'Is there something you would like to tell me about, Isaac?' she asked. Sophia could feel the emotions welling up within her and clamped her lips firmly together to try and stop from blubbering like a small child. Her greatest dream had almost been realised and here before her lay the man she had adored for most of her life and who she had missed for five lonely years. A man she longed for, yet her step-mother had some kind of liaison in the night with him only hours beforehand; a woman who could still face her and eat breakfast and pretend to worry about her future well-being. What was she to think? What explanation could either offer that would be acceptable?

'Come, Sophia. Do not be upset with me. Tell me all quickly and I shall try and explain if there is something amiss.' He raised his hands, palms upwards. 'But you must be quick. You should not be in here.'

'You are here . . . You are here in my home,' she began, but her words were failing her, for to say what she wanted to would incriminate Cynthia and could destroy her family.

'Yes, is that not joyous?' He reached out his hand to her.

'I would have thought so, and I would have thought that this turn of events would have been enough for you . . . that I would have been enough for you.'

Isaac flopped back. 'You are more than I deserve and I could never want a woman more. I have not lived in a stable block these last five years, my love; I have seen the world, life and death and all the horror and beauty in between. I have had you in my heart through battle and peace, through long marches and sieges. Yet here I am stuck by my own body's limitations. My only wish is to be well again and with you for the rest of my life.'

Sophia did not move. 'Your words are well spoken, your sincerity touching, so tell me how could it be possible that you would be able to play me false?'

'You think I would betray our love?'

Sophia could not understand how he was batting her questions back instead of unravelling the secrets of the previous night. Was he playing a game with her? 'Yesterday, I would have said that you were beyond reproach. I would never have doubted you.'

'So why has that changed overnight?' he asked. Sophia watched his features quiver slightly when he mentioned the word 'night'. He nodded slowly, knowingly, as if a puzzle had been solved. 'Did you chance to come here under the cover of darkness, Sophia? Would you have been so bold?'

Sophia felt her cheeks burn. Did he dare to treat her like an ignorant child?

'And what if I did?' she asked, knowing that the truth of it was finally revealed. 'Would that have been such a bad decision, Isaac?'

He stared at her, not shying away from her accusing eyes and instead nodded. 'You accuse an innocent man of a wrongdoing he did not and would never commit.'

'Then what explanation would you give me?' Sophia breathed deeply. 'I would know the truth. I would have you speak to me as an equal. Tell me what occurred!'

'Just believe me when I say that nothing happened that was of any import.'

'That woman came to you in the night! My own stepmother, and you say it was nothing!' Sophia's trembling voice was quiet as she did not wish a servant to overhear, but the fury within each word resonated, nonetheless. 'You tell me what happened! I demand to know!'

'He will not say anymore to you,' a voice from behind her answered. Cynthia was stood there. 'He is an honourable man and you would place him in a situation where, even if the truth were told, it would discredit another lady, for it was I, 'a lady', who came to him!' Cynthia was dressed in her day coat, ready to leave for Gorebeck. 'I have not time to explain now, but trust us both, dear, sweet Sophia. For as guilty as I am for putting a daring test before your young man, you are guiltier than I.'

'How so?' Sophia reacted instantly.

'You would have broken your word to your father and done more than any unmarried, single lady should do. Even now you stand here alone in a bedchamber with Isaac whilst your father is in his study.'

'I —'

'Hush, child. I have a journey to make for our hero. Leave your man alone, before you are discovered with him and he is barred from you forever. And never judge me ill again, for we are friends and as such should trust each other!' Cynthia nodded to Isaac, and then stared back at Sophia. 'I will be back before dinner this evening. Put that petulant lip away!' Cynthia swung around and flounced out of the room, leaving the door open for

Sophia to follow.

'How dare she speak so?' Sophia whispered to Isaac. 'This is my home and you are my father's guest! Her behaviour is —'

'She knows she did something very wrong, but in her mind it was for the best of reasons,' Isaac interrupted. 'Please sit down so that I can give you some explanation.'

Sophia saw the familiar glint return to his eyes and sunk into the chair next to his bed. 'I need to know the truth,' she whispered.

'Yes, you keep demanding it. Very well — listen and I will be quick, for it is this. She wanted to know if I played you false or would take advantage of you. I did neither, so I passed her stupid test. However, she knows about my correspondence with London, and that is why I have had to trust her. This is where I owe you an apology, Sophia; there is more to my story that I have not had the opportunity to share with you.'

Sir Kenneth's voice could be heard

downstairs talking to Cynthia. 'Are you off out, my dear?' he said, quite amiably as Sophia ran over to the landing to listen lest he should climb the stairs.

'Yes, I am going to town. Is there anything that I can fetch back for you?' Cynthia responded, her words light and happy as usual.

'Then we shall join you, Lucas Huntley and I. Where is Sophia? Is she not coming too?'

'She has gone out already for a ride, I believe,' Cynthia said.

'Very well,' he said. 'Brent, have the maid clean my study while I am out and watch she does not disturb my papers.'

Sophia watched them leave from the shadows. She hovered long enough for Brent to disappear down the servants' corridor to the kitchens. She returned to Isaac, this time shutting the door quietly in case a maid should arrive.

His manner seemed jovial.

'I am still angry with her, for her behaviour has been more like that of a courtesan than a respectable wife.'

Sophia, vexed with Cynthia, hoped that her father's heart would be safe in the woman's keeping. There is no fool like an old one, she thought.

'You can trust her, Sophia. Besides, I have good news. I have wealth coming to me — a sizeable sum,' Isaac declared.

'How so?' she asked, surprised by this revelation.

'I was fortunate enough to fall upon some trinkets whilst on reconnaissance. Soldiers often acquire what has been discarded by the enemy. I was very lucky to see something being buried by a Frenchman who could not carry his haul anymore. He obviously intended to return to it when the war was over but he was shot in the following attack. I returned and unearthed his 'treasure'. With some ingenuity and cunning, although I say so myself, I brought it back to England and it has been converted into pounds and shillings. I await the documents to prove that I have these funds available to me from the bankers in Threadneedle Street.'

‘Should this ‘treasure’ not have been handed over to the army and put towards the war effort?’ Sophia asked.

‘No, for it was not taken from a specific place that we were invading. There was no way of knowing who the man was, or why he would leave valuables in a hole in the ground. If he were so careless with it then who am I to question my good fortune in discovering it? Believe me, the money is legitimately mine, but I will only have proof it exists at all once I have the confirmation. I should have gone there to finalise my affairs but I have been detained. I have only to await that letter to advise me that my account is settled. Then I can make my proposition to your father and he will have to view me in a very different light.’ Isaac’s eyes were almost sparkling with joy.

‘But what of its owner?’ Sophia asked. ‘His family may have lost everything . . .’

‘The original owners will be long gone. The French man, who no doubt stole it from someone else, was wearing the uniform of Napoleon. This is war, Sophia.

He died trying to kill my men. You must understand things are very different out there.' Isaac's expression was crestfallen.

'But you do not know this. You could be justifying your own theft by —'

At the word 'theft', Isaac sat bolt upright. 'That money is as much mine as this Hall is your father's.' His colour was high; his hands were pushing down into the bed so that he could sit upright and face her.

Sophia's words had stabbed his heart in some way, but then so had his retort hers. How could he possibly liken the find of a scared man's 'treasure' with the ownership of a grand Hall on an ancient estate such as theirs? Her hand tightened into a fist on her lap.

'Father's birth right meant that he inherited this land from his forefathers. It has been in the family for generations,' Sophia protested. 'You cannot make such a foolish comparison. It is beneath you. You might want to justify your actions, and I can see why you thought this might buy you Father's respect, but stealing is stealing! Even if the man was a thief it does not give you the right to take his possessions from him.'

'Sophia! Think how many slaves' lives went into providing your family's wealth! Please do not judge me for keeping what the good Lord showed me was there for the taking.'

Sophia stood up. 'You judge my family ill.'

'Sophia, think about it. Look at the pictures of your grandfather more closely and his father before him. Do they not show ships in the background, representing trade? Consider what trade that is. You are an intelligent woman. Do you think sheep alone explains such wealth?'

'You speak of what you do not understand. You are bitter because you were born to a stable hand. But I would have accepted you as a stable lad or a lieutenant.' She grabbed her hat and ran down the stairs and through the house to the stables, his words still ringing in her ears. The truth in his words was hard to bear but bear it she must. For what had been said could never be unsaid. Her future had been looking so bright only the day before, but now, whichever way she looked, it was tainted.

The delightful mild-mannered Cynthia had shown herself to be dangerous and calculating. Her father was completely blind to his wife's character, and Isaac . . . He held hidden grudges because of her wealth.

She had never questioned where her family's wealth was from; presuming the money from wool and sheep provided the upkeep along with the tenants' tithes. How naïve she was — of course there was not enough to be gained from that alone to pay for their way of life.

Isaac was right. Her whole world was built on the proceeds of a vile trade and the corruption of men through time. How her heart ached for a simpler way of life. She looked back at Fenton Hall, her home. Why had she never questioned any of it?

She could not change the world, but she would change her life. Cynthia was quite capable of running the house, but she would never bother as long as Sophia was there to do all the tedious parts of her role for her.

'I am no child!' Sophia said to herself. Cynthia could have her world and Sophia would determine her own. It would have Isaac in it, but he would have to accept her as a woman in her own right, not as his prize possession.

22

Lucas Huntley chose to ride alongside the carriage. Sir Kenneth was inside it with Cynthia.

'Did you not want to enjoy the fresh air also, Kenneth?' Cynthia asked.

'I have had enough of riding in saddles of late and will be glad of a seat, even if the journey will be tediously slow.' Sir Kenneth smiled at his wife. Cynthia knew he was well aware of her anxiety and that it would be for the sake of her nerves that he had accompanied her.

The coach lurched as it moved forward and Cynthia grabbed hold of the leather handle of the door. Sir Kenneth reached across her and took her hands in his. He placed them back on her lap and patted them as if placating a child. It was gestures like this that endeared this brusque man to her. He had a good heart. 'You are safe, my dear. I am here sitting right next to you and I will not let any harm happen to us, will I?'

She nodded and sat back. He understood her fear — the crash that had upended the coach her family were travelling in when she was a child had haunted her for decades. Her grandmother had died the next day from the shock of her injuries.

Cynthia nodded back at Sir Kenneth and forced a smile upon her face. No words of explanation were needed, not between them.

'I have been neglecting you, Cynthia,' he declared.

'I always miss you; you know that,' she replied. 'How has your time with Mr Huntley been?' she asked. 'Do you like him?'

'Lucas has a lot of character, a keen wit, and certainly a lot more energy than I do now,' he chuckled. 'Truth be told, he reminds me a little of myself at that age. He has a nose for a good deal and he goes with his instincts. His confidence is infectious.'

'You didn't answer my question, Kenneth,' she repeated.

'Didn't I?' he said, innocently.

'Do you like him?' Cynthia persisted.

'Why, that is simply answered,' he began.

'Then try saying 'yes' or 'no'.' She raised her eyebrows at him. He could be infuriating when he did not wish to commit to a definite answer on something.

'Well, how can I not like him, my dear? If I said I did not, then it would be to admit that I didn't like my younger self, which would be a grave folly, for my past made me what I am today.' He winked at her annoyed expression.

'You play with words,' she said.

He laughed as she pursed her lips.

'I do not think you are that similar to Mr Huntley, Kenneth.' Cynthia glanced out of the window and saw that Lucas Huntley was talking to Robert Judd who was driving the coach.

'No, why not? Has my energy faded so much that I am not even a shadow of my former self?'

'No, you have the energy of a man

years younger than you are. I mean that you knew where to stop following your nose, or your heart, and let your head take over. I do not think Mr Huntley has learnt that yet. There is something far too impetuous about him.'

'Perhaps he has much to learn, but I was not always so wise either.'

'You did not break an engagement, Kenneth,' Cynthia remarked and then bit her lip, but words like air once released could not be expunged.

She was grateful when he changed the subject. 'So, how fares young Dalesman?' he asked.

'Isaac fares well. I suspect that he will be on his crutches when we return. He hates being restrained and cannot tolerate being seen in the basket chair. It hardly goes with the image of a hero,' she explained.

'And Sophia?' he asked.

'Sophia reads to him and entertains both Isaac and Lucas when they are not playing chess. She seems happy enough to have two handsome men to entertain.'

He looked pensively at her. 'So long as that is all she is doing for him — Isaac, that is.'

'Kenneth!' Cynthia shook her head.

'Do not look so shocked, woman. You know their past. Make sure it does not reoccur in their present. A uniform cannot mask the truth of a man's birth. He is personable also, but do not forget where he was born. But enough talk of these young men who have descended upon our peace. I was thinking it is a while since we went to London. We should go there for a month or two.'

Cynthia did not answer. She had no intention of going to London when she had everything she wanted right here. Fresh air was important to her, and she loved her Hall, her small family and their infrequent guests. Why head into the milieu of her past — old connections, shadows of a life she had extricated herself from?

She would not be travelling to the city, but she was well aware that when Sir Kenneth set his mind to a plan, he made it happen. This time she would have to convince him it would be a very bad notion indeed.

23

Sophia surveyed the estate from the edge of the moor road. It was her home, she loved it, but she loved Isaac more. She cantered down the woodland path, slowing when the track narrowed until it opened out across the fields, then she galloped, returning to the Hall.

'Judd!' she called into the stable.

Silence.

She walked her horse into an empty stall and looked around but could see no sign of the stable lad. 'Digby?' she called out, but still there was no response.

She would find Brent; this was not good enough. Where was everyone?

Sophia had only taken two steps outside the building when Digby appeared at her side. He rushed out of the stables behind her.

'Yes, miss,' he said.

'Were you napping?' she asked.

'No, miss, I was sorting stores.'

'See to Betsy and when Judd returns tell him I wish to speak with him.' Sophia did not like being sneaked up on.

'Yes, miss,' he said and ran back into the stable.

Sophia changed out of her riding attire. The realisation that she had stormed off and left a man who could not fend for himself in a house bereft of servants made her feel guilty. She decided to do what she had been brought up to do: put on a brave face and bluff her way through what was yet another awkward situation.

Sophia selected three books from her father's library. One was a description of the Isle of Wight, showing where the exploratory traveller could comfortably stay. The next was a collection of papers and drawings on anatomy, and the third was a book of instruction on the running of a large country estate. Isaac would need that knowledge in time, so Sophia reasoned she had better start preparing him now.

She made her way up the grand

staircase and entered the willow room. Isaac was balanced on the window seat with his leg supported on a cushion; he glanced her way but did not speak to her. He looked as if he had been thinking hard — dismal lines were etched into his forehead.

'Goodness, I hope you did not struggle over there on your own.'

He did not respond.

'Here, Isaac, you may fill your hours in useful pursuit,' she said without sitting down. She placed the books on the small table at his side.

He lifted each one in turn, studying all three covers. 'Does this mean I am forgiven for my ill-timed outburst?' he said quietly, his voice hoarse. 'Am I to forgive you yours, or am I to accept that I am no more than a common thief?' He was still staring at the books as if he did not want to look her in the eyes.

'You said what you thought, you were honest, and I have reflected upon your words. There may be some truth in them, but I am hardly going to apologize for the way the world is and my benefit from it, for I was born into this family, Isaac. You should read this then your understanding of estate management may well improve. If you can separate your conscience from our past, our ignorant forefathers having been involved in the trade, then you can do this. For Father has no connection with that now — I know this because he supports the reformers, led by Mr Wilberforce.'

Isaac nodded his approval. 'And this one?' he said, as he lifted up the small book on the Isle of Wight.

'Seeing as we will not be able to do a tour of Europe when we are wed, we shall honeymoon on the Isle of Wight — Ventnor perhaps, or Shanklin.' She raised one eyebrow as he looked at her and his smile slowly returned to his troubled face.

He laughed. 'Sophia, can I speak to you honestly?'

Sophia nodded.

'I am sorry that I spoke so bluntly. I should have told you straight away that Cynthia was not so innocent or light of wit as you and Robert appear to think she is . . .'

Sophia's eyes widened when he mentioned Robert. He had been gossiping with the servants, which showed up his lack of understanding of his position as their guest.

'I know what you are thinking, Sophia,' Isaac continued, noticing her expression. 'Do not send me back to the stables with my ignorant head in my hands. Robert is a servant, but we were friends back then and we are still now. More than friends; when Father took him on it was like having a brother.' He sighed, and continued, 'Your father is a good man and one who I am grateful to a thousand times over. However, you really did speak out about things that you have no understanding of. That man who hid his treasure had clearly looted it from somewhere. Besides, there would be no chance to repatriate the people, if they still breathed, with their valuables. How then was I to pass by? As you said, I could have handed them over to a superior officer who would have lined his already well fed coffers further. Sometimes in life you have to seize the blessings that lay before you. War is not all black and white. Horrendous wrongs are done on all sides, so if out of the ashes something good can grow, let it. I did not steal or kill for it. I merely retrieved it.'

'Your apologies are accepted but be careful what you tell your friend Robert. He may not be as trustworthy as you think. He seems to be jealous of you already, so say nothing of your secret fortune to him.' Sophia was certain she spoke the truth.

'Sophia, please stop and think a minute. Who is it that knows the world below stairs better? Would it be you, or me? Could it possibly be that your head is filled with upstairs presumptions of what goes on below?' He tilted his head to one side as if it would soften the cut of his words. It did not.

Sophia sniffed. 'You make a very good point, Isaac, but you also may well be naïve because you have been away for years and now this friend who was equal to you is now serving you. I am sure that you have confided in Judd that we are still in love, and that is dangerous.' Isaac coloured slightly and that confirmed her suspicions.

'My family does not exist anymore, Sophia. Mrs Gribbins, who has had firm words in my ear about our clandestine visits, along with Robert, are as dear to me as my own father was. How can I act superior to them? How can I think they would turn against me?' He shook his head. 'I cannot in my heart, for I know I am not their better, just more fortunate than they have been.'

'Then be yourself and stop apologising for it. But do not tell them anything else until Mr Huntley is out of our lives and Father accepts your business proposal. Isaac, Judd was thwarted in love when the girl he wanted to propose to married another — he will see all of God's blessings falling your way and few his. I tell you he has a jealous streak; this is why the girl married another. He spends far too much time in the inn in Gorebeck.'

'And how would you know all this servants' gossip?' he asked.

She winked at him. 'Because I once was not too proud to befriend a servant, if you recall.'

'Oh, I see, you ignore your father's orders. So who do you befriend now?' He smiled. 'Very well, keep your secret. I will heed your warning.'

'Now, tell me, why did you trust Cynthia to collect your letter, and not me?'

Isaac stared at her. 'Sophia, I should have trusted you with the task, but I did not wish to burden you further and risk your father's wrath if you should have been discovered.' He shook his head. 'I sought only to protect you and your reputation.'

Sophia did not wish to pursue the matter further. Isaac was hers and that was all that mattered. She nestled his head to her bosom. 'Oh, Isaac, what fools we are! We must be more careful.'

'Perhaps embracing me by the window is not the best way to be prudent,

Sophia.' Isaac laughed as she took a step backwards. 'Sophia, if I have true wealth, I will need that head of yours to be at its sharpest for I am not used to it. You will have to be my guide and my partner in all things. I have no wish to gamble, squander, or flaunt it, but to use it to secure our future so we shall never be poor, and when Napoleon is defeated, which he will be, we shall celebrate with my limited 'family' and make their lives more amenable too.' He reached out and drew her near to him, taking her hand in his own.

'You are a good man, Lieutenant Dalesman, and I love you as much as I always have.' Sophia kissed his fingers delicately and wished that she could walk him over to the bed. Isaac grimaced and she watched his expression. Had he shifted his weight awkwardly to reposition his sore leg?

'Sorry,' Sophia said. 'Have I hurt you?' she asked, looking along at his leg.

He smiled up at her. 'I am fine — it was just a warning pang to ask you to release me.'

She took a step away from him, laughing. 'Isaac, read your books and I will go and see to my duties. I may be here to advise you as to how to manage your wealth but, as the man, you will have to deal with things.'

* * *

Sophia had much to think about. She enlisted the services of a junior maid who rarely came above stairs to reorganise her clothes and sort her chest of drawers. This innocent act, which was passed off as an opportunity for the girl to expand her knowledge in the absence of the upper housemaids, meant that Sophia had two complete outfits to hand to pack in a trice: one for day wear and one for travel. Then, should she need to leave at short notice, she would be prepared without Cynthia's or the servants' knowledge.

Isaac would not be able to travel for some time, but if her avoiding a match meant removing herself to Beckton Abbey for a short time, then she would. The nuns had always been kind to her when she arranged for the excess produce from the Hall's gardens to supplement their own when needed. She received extra herbs and honey from them as a thank you.

The carriage returned later that afternoon with Cynthia alone. Sophia watched its painfully slow progress up the drive. Cynthia alighted, relieved and smiling, with the help of Robert Judd.

'I shall need a nice warm drink to calm my nerves, Sophia,' she declared and continued to complain bitterly that the vehicle shook her to her bones no matter what pace it travelled at. 'You never know when those animals might become overly excited and bolt.'

Sophia walked out to greet Cynthia pleasantly enough. They exchanged a warm welcome as if nothing had happened earlier between them.

'I hope your journey was pleasant,' Sophia said awkwardly.

'Yes, as much as torture could ever be.' Cynthia sniffed as she took off her hat and gloves.

Sophia laughed, because Cynthia's exaggeration was playful.

'Your father will return later with Lucas Huntley. How is our wounded soldier?' Cynthia asked.

'Impatient to be up and about,' Sophia replied honestly. 'Perched on the window seat, I understand.'

'Good, I will instruct Brent that tomorrow he and Judd must make him presentable first thing and fetch him down to the morning room for breakfast and he can join us for the whole day. Then he can sit by the patio windows if it is another warm day and be entertained by your charming playing on the pianoforte for a while. Afterwards the men can chat amongst themselves, whilst we retire, and plan the menus for the coming week. It is time we gave Mrs Gribbins a greater challenge, I feel. It should make for a pleasant afternoon.'

'Did you collect the post?' Sophia

asked.

'Yes,' Cynthia replied, but said no more as she ascended the stairs.

24

Sophia was glancing out of the window of the morning room when her father and Lucas Huntley returned. She could not help but admire Mr Huntley's poise. Confidence exuded from his every step and gesture. There was no doubt he was a fine figure of a man. She went to greet them as they entered the stable yard. The day was warm and sunny, so it was good to step outside.

'You are a vision of perfection, as always,' Lucas Huntley greeted her, as he dismounted, leading his horse to where Digby was waiting to take the reins. Robert Judd was coming to meet them also. Lucas had no need of the mounting block, slipping his left leg out of the stirrup, he casually swung it over the side of the saddle and freed his right boot gliding with ease to the floor, landing square. Her father dismounted, using the block as Robert Judd held the horse's bit steady.

'And you are too generous with your compliments as always, sir,' she replied. It was hard not to show that his attention humoured her.

'That is why you are so becoming; you really believe that I exaggerate the truth.' He looked to the sky and then back to her eyes as if he was amazed by her modesty.

Sophia shook her head. As always, he had the correct response to her comments. She liked his quick wit; it meant that she could spar with him easily, which had passed many an hour whilst Isaac lay bored in bed.

'I have had fresh lemonade served in the orangery,' Sophia said, as her father joined them. 'Cynthia returned an hour ago, Father.'

'Good God, she could have got out and walked alongside it quicker!' He shook his head. 'The lemonade is a lovely thought, but you two go ahead. I will join you shortly,' he said and patted her arm before walking into the Hall.

'It appears we have been abandoned,'

Lucas said.

'Miss, you wanted to see me,' Robert Judd interrupted, rather too abruptly, Sophia thought.

'Yes, leave the horses to Digby and tend to Lieutenant Dalesman. He may wish to join us.'

Robert Judd nodded, but his eyes bore into hers.

'Go on, man,' Lucas said.

Sophia saw the instant obedience as Robert Judd replied, 'Yes, sir,' and headed straight for the kitchen doorway.

Sophia bristled. How dare Judd respond more quickly to a guest than her? If his attitude continued she would speak to her father . . . but that thought stopped dead in his tracks as she realised she could not. Judd knew too much about her and Isaac.

Lucas cut through her thoughts. 'May I suggest that we take a turn around the walled garden first and enter the orangery from the outside rather than going back through the dusky old Hall?' Lucas offered. 'It is such a beautiful day after all, and I am sure you are tired of hiding away within it on such a day as this.'

She hesitated.

'Go on, I dare you to feel the sun caress those beautiful cheeks.' He gestured towards the walled garden that ran the length of the Hall's west side from front to back and then joined the orangery at one corner.

'What a splendid idea,' Sophia agreed, for she could not see the harm in it. His words were more poetic than those Isaac used, even though they were empty of sincerity by comparison. He was a man who had been schooled and preened to be a gentleman, not a stable hand or soldier, and he knew how to enjoy life. But then when one was born and bred to such a life, funded by either old or new money, it was wealth you knew and expected.

Isaac had been raised well, but to a world of toil, and only learnt his letters by reading the Bible. It was no surprise that he still lacked social graces. Isaac was to be complimented for he had done well as one from the lower orders. It could hardly compare with such a man's education as Mr Huntley or her father's.

Lucas stepped aside, so that Sophia could lead the way into the shelter of the garden by the old wooden gateway. Inside the garden were immaculately laid beds of flowers and vegetables making such a pleasing sight to view.

Sophia heard the gates being latched behind her and glanced back. Lucas Huntley was walking along the outer path that followed the wall around the rectangular flower beds. She was going to go straight to the orangery through the centre of the garden to be clearly visible from the Hall, but Lucas stopped her.

'Let us take the air and enjoy the day a little longer. We can walk the full circuit. After all, it is so rare that we can talk to each other with any privacy.' He breathed deeply. 'Ah, pure air, so far away from the city stench — perfect! That will be what Australia will be like — fresh, unspoilt beauty just as are you, my dear Sophia.'

Sophia glanced around them, ignoring his remark, but liking it nonetheless. His comments were often surprising if not slightly odd to her, and he intrigued her. With the Hall overlooking the gardens, and despite the fact that there were no gardeners working at that particular hour, she could not see any harm in doing as he said, so she began walking on the outer path. Each plot was edged with narrow oak slabs where the beds alternated between beautiful flowers, lobelias, roses and nasturtiums, seasonal vegetables, not to mention the profusion of strawberry plants.

'So what have you been up to with Father these past few days?' she asked.

'He has been showing me his stock of sheep, as well as talking of his horses.' Lucas walked slightly ahead of her, standing in the shade of the arbour. 'He really has an impressive selection of bloodlines going back generations, in both cases. I think we will be able to make a really good arrangement, Sophia. He has exactly what I want to own, and when a Huntley sets their heart on something — it invariably happens.' His eyes were admiring her in a perceptibly personal way. He reached up and picked a wild pink rose that was woven across the frame of honeysuckle. As Sophia entered the shade he presented the flower to her with a flourish of a bow that would have made any dandy proud.

Sophia giggled — just like Cynthia would, she thought, as she dipped a curtsey and reached out for it. But as she did so, he took hold of her fingers, letting the flower drop to the ground, and led her deeper into the middle of the fragrant tunnel. Sophia laughed but, three steps into the shade, she realised they were completely hidden from the view from the Hall. Even if they were watched from a window, they would not be seen in this sheltered spot. Her father had warned her against this.

She pulled away, wanting to retrace her steps, but he did not release his grip.

'We must join my father and Cynthia in the orangery,' Sophia said, and tried to step past him, but he encircled her waist with his arms and gently brought her close into a firm embrace.

'Mr Huntley!' she gasped. 'What do you think you are doing?'

Her words were lost to him, smothered by his lips; a moist, eager mouth so keen to devour her that she was silenced by his actions. Panic rose — he was stealing her breath. Her chest heaved as she struggled with his arms, using her hands to push them away. If they were caught she realised she would be trapped — her father would never believe her again, and could force a union with Mr Huntley upon her.

Lucas loosened his grip on her and allowed Sophia to stand up straight again, steadying her as she stared at him. She was repulsed by his actions, and yet he still held on to her hands. She tugged hard to try and free them.

'You shame both yourself and me, sir!' Sophia exclaimed, and continued to try to free her hands from his, but his grip was firm.

‘No, my pretty Sophia. I merely give you a taste of me, a promise of the delights that you and I will experience together.’ He let her hands drop and casually gestured they should continue their walk. ‘Should we?’

‘I do not understand what you mean,’ she said, ‘nor do I wish to!’ Sophia brushed her skirts down with the palms of her hands so that they did not appear at all crushed or creased by his assault. No one must know of this and she would make sure he never had the opportunity to compromise her again. Lucas had shown his true colours and she her gullibility — no, stupidity!

‘I think you do, Sophia, for you cover your tracks well.’ He gestured to her actions. ‘Rather than run screaming to your father for my ungentlemanly behaviour, you are more concerned about your appearance and what it might reveal to him about what we have been doing.’ He laughed at her indignant expression. ‘You give yourself away, my dear. You may well not be as innocent as he thinks, for you neither faint nor flee!'

His grin was wide. Was he openly laughing at her? She did not care for his manner or inference. Yes, he was correct, her actions were not that of a frightened maid and that was to her shame. She quickened her step, her thoughts muddled. Lucas stopped her again by holding her right arm above the elbow in his left hand.

'Calm yourself down, my dear — give yourself a moment for the excitement to subside and breathe deeply. I want a warm blooded woman, so you will not disappoint. Do not worry, I shall not tell your father.'

Sophia needed to be calm. 'Let go of me before I do say something that will destroy your reputation further and ruin your business arrangements with Father.' She glared at him, defiant, and resolved not to show fear — any more than she may have already.

'There is no need for threats.' He looked at her curiously for one moment. 'You are aware that my reputation has a dent in it. That is interesting. So you care enough for me to have bothered to find out if there is a stain on my character,' he said and looked even more humoured.

'It is common knowledge that you deserted your fiancé,' she accused him and saw the smile fade. So, she thought, he was sensitive to it, but obviously thought that they were so far removed from his usual society that she would not know of his shame.

'Is it?' he murmured and looked slightly taken aback. 'Your mama should have told you not to listen to idle gossip,' he scolded her. 'But stuck out in this wasteland I suppose you have to find something to fill in the hours.'

'I listen to facts,' she railed. 'Cynthia is not my mama.'

'Very well, did she also tell you why I did this 'terrible thing'?' He cocked his head on one side.

She hesitated.

'No, of course she would not because only I and the lady in question actually know the truth of it. So as it is nobody else's business other than ours I will not bother your ears. I know too well how ladies like to gossip.' He folded his arms across his chest and stared down at her.

She wanted to strike his arrogant face, but suspected that, if she did, this man whose passions ran so high would certainly do likewise, even if it brought him more shame and lost her father's favour. He was impetuous — too impetuous.

'You insult me in an unfair and cruel way, sir,' she said.

'I did not mean to insult you at all.' He shrugged. 'It is my way, Sophia. I am a man who speaks his mind, and I go all out to have what I want in life. I have no doubt that you are as a maid should be, and I am glad that you are not weak in nature or given to a fit of the vapours. I need a woman who has a strong character and bearing, who can accept a full and active married life. You are that woman. So —' he stood aside — 'let us rejoin the family, composed and in a friendly way, for we do not want to upset them, do we? Rather than have you rushed into a marriage through our shameful actions, let us do it with the good will of both our fathers.'

'That is no way to behave to a lady, and one who you should be showing a great deal of respect to. I am not part of Father's ancient stock or blood line to be bought at auction!' She walked on.

'I like that spirit. Try to convince yourself of that, Sophia, if you can, for you are the bloodline that will continue the heritage of this estate, but I respect you for who you are, Sophia.' He raised his voice slightly. 'You will need it where our lives are destined to go. And do not fear the rest, for I look after what is mine well enough. You shall always be protected and provided for, and I shall never neglect you. We will have a full and active marriage, my dear.'

'My destiny will not be dictated to me by a man who would steal kisses in an arbour!' She quickened her step.

'Not yet, my sweet, but soon,' he said and then appeared in step at her side, so when they could be seen in the daylight they were to be walking together. 'Admit it at least to yourself, Sophia — you found my kisses exciting,' he said to her under his breath.

'I admit nothing!' Sophia said in response, trying not to look alarmed at his words. The man had no limit to his arrogance.

'You do not deny it either, though,' he replied whilst waving to Cynthia who had had the manservant open the orangery doors to admit them both.

There was not time for her to formulate an answer, which was just as well as there was none she could give. Deep inside, she knew that the answer was — yes, it had been intoxicating, but it had also been dangerous, not loving. To compare his assault with Isaac's sensuous touch was unfair. There simply was no comparison. Besides, one was recovering from a wound, the other was fit and in good health.

Lucas was right, his action showed he promised more of the same. If he would be like that on his first intimate moment, she knew then he would not be at all considerate of her feelings in the future. He had said it himself, 'Huntleys took what they wanted'. Where was the love in that?

Sophia remembered all too well the heightened feelings that Isaac aroused in her every time they were intimate. He did not grip her, but held her in a warm embrace.

She re-entered the shade of the orangery and was aware of Cynthia studying her as the men talked about Isaac's recovery.

'He will be joining us shortly,' her father announced.

Cynthia clapped her gloved hands together. 'That is such good news.' She smiled at Sophia who merely nodded back in a gesture of acknowledgement and carefully poured herself a glass of lemonade whilst trying to stifle the wave of indignation that still consumed her. She did not spill one drop and so did not give her feelings away, despite Lucas Huntley's intense stare.

'Good morning, Lieutenant.' Cynthia welcomed Isaac as he appeared in the doorway on crutches, helped by Robert Judd. He looked fresh and wore one of Sir Kenneth's burgundy silk dressing gowns. It suited him very well, Sophia thought.

'You must join us for some light refreshment, Lieutenant,' Cynthia remarked and gestured for Robert Judd to help seat Isaac.

Robert helped Isaac and then was swiftly dismissed by Brent, who stood back against the wall and oversaw the food being brought in on platters by two maids.

Sophia was taken aback by the dark look that Robert Judd cast her as he passed her by. The man was objectionable. Had he seen Lucas and her in the arbour? She breathed in quickly and glanced at Brent's impassive face as their eyes exchanged silent words before Robert left. He too seemed to stand in judgement upon her. My goodness, how she wished that Isaac was her acknowledged beau, then they would know to bury their stupid prejudices.

25

After a light repast Isaac was looking very weary and insisted that a nap in his chair would be sufficient rest, instead of returning to his bedchamber.

Sophia realised he had had enough of the polite conversation and left him to his peace. Cynthia decided to take a turn around the garden with Lucas Huntley, so Sophia slipped away, entering the study.

'Father, I need to talk to you,' she said as she approached.

Sir Kenneth was seated at his desk with his head down, lost to his thoughts.

'Why, what have you done now?' he said in a very serious voice, but then when he glanced up at her he smiled. He was merely teasing her.

'Nothing that I should not have, Father.' Her reply was light and cheerful but a pang of guilt gnawed at her, as where Isaac was concerned she had indeed done more than she should have, and willingly. 'It is about your plans with Mr Huntley, Father,' she began. What that man had done to her she did not dare reveal to her father in case he presumed the fault lay with her.

'Indeed, that is strange as I was going to talk to you about the very same. So we are in an accord for once. Who do you think should go first?' He waited for her response.

Sophia was keen to jump in, but for once in her life she didn't. Instead, she smiled sweetly back at him and said, 'Father, you must of course, but I would ask that you then listen seriously to my comments and consider them please.' She had never felt so dutiful in her life; perhaps some of Cynthia's advice was beginning to wear off on her as she also felt strangely in control.

'Very well, that seems fair to me.' He nodded and gestured to her that she should sit opposite him.

Sophia did, but instantly felt small in the large leather chair. Perhaps that was his intention as she noticed that his seating seemed elevated by comparison to hers.

'Please, begin, Father,' she said and, instead of sitting upright and awkward in this reduced position, she nestled comfortably back. One thing Sophia knew she must do was to keep her temper. This conversation could make or destroy her and Isaac's dreams. Sophia listened attentively to every word her father uttered.

'Old Mr Huntley is a life-long friend of Cynthia's family and I have known them as associates on occasional visits to London for years. As such, they have my hospitality and utter respect.'

Sophia nodded. 'I appreciate that. Old friends are very precious.' She was meaning with Isaac; her father gave no indication that her words had a special message to hand deliver.

'They have a plan to raise a vast number of sheep on land they are purchasing in Australia. That country has a very different climate to our own, presenting a challenging environment, so I understand. They are people of opportunity and do not hesitate to go with a new venture. Charles Huntley has been very successful in his business dealings in the past. He is very keen to move his venture along, as the purchase of their acreage has been approved. It seems he wishes to send Lucas out there to oversee the initial arrivals and set up the farm. He will need good strong hands as well as the beasts themselves. He is not short of confidence and is able.' Her father stopped and sat still, staring at her.

She nodded at him, her lips clenched tight, so much so that they ached. Her Isaac would be strong and able again and he did not need to travel to the other side of the world to prove it. Sophia knew he would make a full recovery.

'Sophia, unless you have become struck down with some affliction that cannot prevent your head from rocking like a nursery horse, then please stop it!' He placed the palms of both his hands down on the desk and she realised he would finish the conversation there and then if she didn't speak up.

'Sorry, Father,' she said and sat upright with her fingers interlocked on her lap. 'I was listening to your words with great interest; they are important to me.'

'I realise that. So when did you have this change of persona?' He sighed. 'Do not play games with me.'

'I have listened to you as you have told me on many occasion that I should do,' she said sweetly.

He shook his head and continued. 'So tell me, what is your impression of Mr Lucas Huntley so far?' he asked her, and this time it was he who sat back, his chin resting on his interlocking forefingers of his hands.

'He is quick of wit, confident and makes every effort to be charming to me,' she answered honestly. 'He thinks I, like your sheep, am hardy and capable of surviving the crossing to this raw land and no doubt breeding him strong heirs, in time.' She was being her usual very blunt self.

Her father raised a brow at her choice of words. 'You are not as young as . . .'

'I do not think he wants a younger woman, Father, but someone who is more mature and in good health.' She held her chin high, trying not to launch into a frustrated tirade of just what she thought of being likened to the stock's bloodline. The feel of Lucas Huntley's lips over her mouth had begun to haunt her. It had been suffocating and she longed for Isaac to remove the memory as only he could. 'And I am certainly of an age to be able to give him sons — which he desires.'

'He does, does he? And when did he have the opportunity to share these thoughts with you?' Sir Kenneth asked and leaned forwards. 'How dare any man speak to you in such a way?' he muttered.

'Earlier, Father, when we walked in the walled garden.' Again, she answered honestly.

'Do you concur with them?' he asked.

'No, Father, for I have no wish to venture so far away from you, Cynthia or my home. Besides . . .'

'Besides, what?' His brow furrowed.

'Besides, he does not love me in the slightest. I believe he finds me attractive for the money that would come to him upon my wedding and down to him in time as your heiress.' She softened her voice for the last comment.

'Love!' Sir Kenneth sighed. 'Always love first with women.' He shook his head.

'Yes, because if we are to submit our lives . . . our body to the will of a man then love at least makes our futures palatable.' Sophia bit her lip because the passion of her words was beginning to show.

'Woman, do not lecture me! You speak of what you should have no knowledge of. Man was put on this planet to look after a woman and she was placed here to obey him in all things and raise children. You, Sophia, would do well to remember that, for you are far too knowledgeable for a maid!'

'I did not mean to upset you, sir,' she

said automatically when his tone hardened.

'You were doing so well, Sophia, yet I am 'sir' again. Never mind, you may go.' He waved her away.

Sophia felt a wave of panic rise. He had found out what he wanted to, her opinion of Lucas Huntley, but she had no understanding of her father's intentions. This, like her life, was not fair!

'Father, what do you intend to do?' she asked, and leaned onto the desk, her eyes moist. Her resolve to remain detached and calm hung in ruins.

He stroked her cheek with one finger. 'Sophia, I will do what I always do. I will look to the future and what is best for you. That is all I have ever done.' He stood up. 'Go and read to the lieutenant and I congratulate you on your control, for not once was Dalesman mentioned as a reason to prevent the marriage to Mr Huntley. You are learning well from my dear Cynthia.'

'Father!' Sophia was going to step towards him, but he put a hand up and waved her away more vehemently.

'Go, Sophia, do not say more to me now or you may work against your own interests, and do not repeat anything of this conversation to anyone else. Do something you rarely have done in the past and trust in me and my judgement. Not another word!'

* * *

Sophia walked out of the Hall and leaned against a column, breathing in the fresh air deeply. Could she trust her own father? She needed more time. Isaac must heal and they had to slow Lucas Huntley and his plans down. But how?

She looked to the sky as if seeking divine intervention. Then she remembered the letter and the promise of Isaac's new money. Would it sway her father's mind? After all, they had so much already — they did not need Isaac's money, but it may prove him worthy in her father's eyes.

Sophia's thoughts were interrupted by a rider coming at a gallop down the drive. Whatever was the matter now? She waited until he dismounted before addressing him. The man seemed exhausted as he made his way up the steps toward her.

'Goodness, man! Whatever brings you here in such haste?' she asked.

'I have an urgent message for a Lieutenant Dalesman,' he said, and pulled out a leather bound wallet from his pockets. A red ribbon tied it firm.

'Thank you, I shall give it to him. You can go.' Sophia held out her hand to receive it, anxious to know if this was the proof of Isaac's good fortune arriving. If so, it was the quickest answer to a prayer she had ever heard of.

He looked apologetically at her through a very tired face. 'I'm sorry, miss, but I have been instructed to give it to him directly.'

'Really, I am the daughter of this estate. You can trust it to my care.'

'I would without question if it were

mine, but it is more than my employment is worth, ma'am, not to carry out my instruction to the letter.'

'Then follow me!' she ordered. 'Brent!' she shouted as she re-entered the Hall, not at all happy that she had been rebuffed.

'Yes, Miss Sophia.' He walked briskly out of the library.

'Have Judd see to this man's horse!' she ordered.

Brent stared directly back at her. 'Yes, miss.' His mouth reset in its normal tight line.

She ignored his brusque tone; all these years and still she was never comfortable in his presence. She showed the rider to a seat in the hallway. 'Wait here.'

Sophia found Isaac playing chess in the orangery with Lucas Huntley. Cynthia was resting on the chaise longue. Her father, she presumed, was still in the study.

'Lieutenant Dalesman, you are needed in the hallway.' Sophia saw the curious look upon Lucas Huntley's face, but

Isaac did not question her and stood up, using his crutches to regain his balance.

'Very well,' he said, adding, 'I shall return soon, Lucas.'

'Take your time, man, whilst I discover a tyrannical move that will lose you your king. My queen is crying out for revenge.' Lucas smiled but his eyes were transfixed on the game before him.

Isaac laughed.

Cynthia's eyes closed again as he passed by her but Sophia knew she would be very curious to know why Sophia should call Isaac away from them so openly.

Isaac and Sophia cut through the morning room. 'There is a man with a document wallet waiting for you. He came post haste. Who is he, Isaac?' she asked quietly. 'Will it be from your London agents?'

'If I am right, it may well be one part of the information I have been waiting for to present to your father. Keep Mr Huntley in the orangery if you can, and leave me time to find out what this man has brought.' He glanced down at her and saw her disapproving expression.

'Very well,' Sophia snapped, feeling as though yet again she had been dismissed and excluded from the business affairs of men. 'Although I do not wish to sit with Mr Huntley.'

'I will explain all later,' Isaac said. 'I promise.'

Sophia nodded and returned to the orangery.

26

'You have an urgent delivery for me?' Isaac said, as he approached the man.

The rider instantly stood up and handed Isaac the documents. 'Mr Entwhistle thanks you for your timely intervention, sir. He assures you that all concerned are greatly relieved.'

'Good, give him my thanks on your return. I hope we shall have no further reason to communicate upon the issue again. Now, if you go through that door —' Isaac lifted a crutch and pointed to the servants' door — 'follow your nose to the kitchens and tell the cook, Mrs Gribbins, that I asked for you to be fed before you return.'

'Thank ye, sir,' the man said, doffed his hat and scooted at speed down the servants' corridor.

Balancing on his crutch, Isaac turned towards the library, where he hoped to be able to read the contents of his delivery unobserved before he laid it before Sir Kenneth. However, standing in the doorway of his study was Sir Kenneth, watching him curiously.

'Sir.' Isaac was taken by surprise and for a second lost his grip, the leather bound file slipping from his hand to the floor where it slid on the tiles to a place a few feet from his own.

Sir Kenneth strode over and retrieved it for him. He looked at it carefully. Isaac had no reason to feel guilty, but he had wanted to read the contents and decide when and where would be the best time and place to front Sir Kenneth. Now that choice had gone.

'Are you receiving despatches here, Lieutenant? Have you been given a further promotion?'

'No, sir, it concerns a delicate matter, that may or may not be of concern to you, but I think it will be of great interest. If we could speak openly in the quiet of your study, I would like to explain further.'

Sir Kenneth raised both eyebrows. 'I

am intrigued. It was good of me to feed the rider food from my kitchens, wasn't it?'

'I know you to be a fair man, sir, and the rider had travelled hard to make it here in such a short time,' Isaac explained.

Sir Kenneth shook his head dismissively. 'Come to my study then and explain what this mystery is about.' Sir Kenneth carried the delivery and led the way inside the room. 'Speak, man!' he said as soon as Isaac shut the door.

'When I was in Gorebeck, visiting Father's grave, a man approached me thinking that I was Lucas Huntley. He was extremely agitated and tried to serve a demand from the man's creditors. His name was Mr Philip Entwhistle, a Sherriff's Officer, who has been chasing Mr Huntley from Newcastle, trying to serve the demand,' Isaac explained.

'How is this of any import to you?' Sir Kenneth had coloured.

Isaac realised this could so easily go bad for him if he bruised Sir Kenneth's pride . . . again. 'I found out that Mr

Huntley was one step away from being thrown into a debtor's lock up. Once in such a place his debt would increase daily until someone could buy him out.'

Sir Kenneth shifted uneasily in his chair. 'I am well aware of how the system works, although I have never had first-hand knowledge of it. So how did you get involved and why have you not mentioned this to Lucas himself?' Sir Kenneth asked.

'Because he is a guest of this family and so I wanted to seek your advice first. The papers in there should list a full account of his debt to these people and also a date by which it must be paid in its entirety. He wants to outrun them by leaving England for Australia. Even if he did it would keep mounting until he was chased across the ocean. The net is closing on him, sir.'

'Yes! Yes! You have made your point very clear. May I?' Sir Kenneth asked as he opened the letter. 'Have you any idea of the amounts listed here?' Sir Kenneth stared at Isaac.

'Yes, sir. I understand they amount to over forty guineas.'

'Goddamn it!' Sir Kenneth turned away from Isaac and stared out of the window at his lands. 'So you expect me to clear them for him, is that it?' Sir Kenneth said, his hands pushed deep into his pockets.

'If you wish to, sir. Whoever pays this debt owns the debt and Mr Huntley becomes indebted to them. He could still find a way to repay that person. The family are friends of yours and I intervened to prevent him being imprisoned.'

'Yes, Isaac Dalesman, I can read. Can you?' he spat the words out as he turned and faced Isaac.

Isaac was steadily balanced upon his crutches. 'Yes, sir, you know I can for you often saw my father teach me from the good book.'

'Yes, well, forgive me that outburst, for I know you to be a good man, but you are still . . .'

'A lieutenant, sir.'

'Leave the matter with me,' Sir Kenneth said. 'I will sort this out between Entwhistle's clients and Mr Huntley, and you must say nothing of it. One fact of life you may be unaware of, Dalesman, is that gentlemen have debts. It is not unusual that a simple oversight can lead to misunderstandings.'

'Sir, I may have been raised in a stable by a humble, God-fearing man but I have lived amongst the rank and file, and drank in the officers' clubs and seen how gentlemen can accrue debt on words of honour, yet when a common man striving to feed their family steals food they can be transported for owing a few unpaid coins.' Isaac stopped before he was accused of being a revolutionary and thrown out of the Hall.

'Dalesman,' Sir Kenneth began to speak but hesitated.

'Yes, sir,' Isaac said and stepped toward the door.

Sir Kenneth sat on the edge of his desk. 'We know about the debtors' note, but Mr Huntley does not, so what good will it do? Unless of course you wish me to discredit him — is that why you intervened, Isaac, to put the man down in my eyes and Sophia's?'

Isaac's hand tightened upon the handle of the door. 'Sir, I thought you should know the nature of the man you have under your roof.' He realised that his words were bold.

'Oh, Isaac, I am well aware of the nature of the people under my roof. Do not think me such a fool. So be honest, man, are you intending to purchase my favour for the price of this debtors' note?'

'It is a fair question, sir.' Isaac looked at him. 'I would ask that you allow me to stay here until, as Doctor Aimes stated, I can walk unheeded again and, if I still do not impress you by my behaviour or circumstance, then I will purchase a higher commission if the wars drag on and prove my love for Sophia all over again.' Isaac's words were calm, for he had wanted to say this to Sir Kenneth since arriving. He wanted the man to know that very soon he would be able to buy a commission, or a home and a myriad of things, but the only thing he wanted could never be bought and that was Sir Kenneth's blessing and Sophia's hand in marriage.

'By God, you are a dreamer if ever I saw one! Be gone and keep word of this to yourself. Do not confide in the women, or I will not be so forgiving and never, ever, presume to preach to me again!'

Isaac nodded, deciding he would try one last time. 'Sir Kenneth there is another matter that I must . . .'

A knock on the door interrupted Isaac's words and as it opened he had to manoeuvre quickly not to be knocked over by Brent's entrance.

'Sir, your horse is made ready and Mr Huntley awaits your pleasure.' Brent glanced at Isaac, curiosity brimming from his eyes.

'Is he indeed? Very well, Dalesman was just leaving.'

Isaac knew that his opportunity was gone. He would have to find another time to talk further of his good fortune. Sir Kenneth's pride had taken a big enough blow for one day.

27

Cynthia and Sophia watched Lucas Huntley and her father ride at a pace in the direction of Gorebeck.

'What was delivered, Sophia?' Cynthia asked.

'An important letter for Isaac. I know no more than you about its contents.' Sophia did not have to lie.

'How irksome that must be for you,' Cynthia said and laughed, not able to keep up the pretence of being aloof.

Sophia could not help but smile at her. 'You have a wicked sense of humour.' Sophia looked upon the woman next to her and realised just how much of a friend she had become. 'I am sorry, Cynthia, if I doubted your intentions with Isaac. It is just that . . .'

'You were expecting to have a night with your injured hero and instead your wicked stepmother dared to enter his bedchamber and question him.'

Sophia blushed.

'Oh, Sophia, you are a woman in love. Do not punish yourself more. Thank me though, for if your night had played out as you had wanted it to, you would have been discovered by your father. My Kenneth is no fool. But, by the way he is riding that horse, I think he is a vexed one. Go seek out that man of yours and find out what has transpired. I need to know if you two lovers are to have a happy ending to your story.'

Sophia squeezed Cynthia's hand and then went in search of Isaac.

* * *

After searching the downstairs rooms, Sophia decided that Isaac would not have gone up to his bedchamber and so she entered the servants' corridor, making her way down to the kitchens. It was a strange feeling of déjà vu for she had not ventured along here since the day she ran away from her mama's screams.

It was colder in this part of the house

than she remembered it. The bare stone walls and flagstone floor held a chill of their own. She closed her eyes momentarily as the images of that night flashed before them. Her senses could feel the fear, even now. Forcing herself to pass the very spot where she had been caught and carried away over Brent's shoulder, she breathed deeply. The past had gone and she desperately wanted to live in the present. Sophia also recalled the heartbreak that had been on Isaac's face and the very different look in Judd's eyes.

She heard light-hearted chatter amongst the clatter of pots and pans being moved around in the kitchen ahead and so put her memories aside and headed straight to their source. One voice was undeniably that of Mrs Gribbins, the other was unmistakably that of Isaac. She entered under the low stone arch and was greeted by the shocked faces of the two maids working between the sink and table.

'Keep working, girls, I have not come down here to rebuke anyone,' Sophia said politely.

The girls did, adding extra vigour to their tasks, which made Sophia smile; they, at least, were obviously in awe of her presence.

Isaac was seated by the fire with a warmed jug of mulled wine in his hand.

Mrs Gribbins lifted her head and smiled. 'You caught me reminiscing with the brave lieutenant here. Sorry, miss,' she said. It was the first time they had spoken to each other since their meeting during the night.

'I am sure that you have much to catch up with.' Sophia looked at Isaac, who appeared to be well warmed through by the side of the open fireplace. 'Were you feeling cold?' she asked him, trying not to show undue concern. He looked in very good health, if it were not for the presence of his crutches leaning against the chair he was sitting in.

'No, not at all, but seeing as you were chatting to Cynthia I thought I would catch up with Mrs Gribbins and so I made my way down the servants' corridor, hoping to also have a moment with Robert.'

'Robert's been busy, lad,' Mrs Gribbins said, but there was an edge to her voice that Sophia could not understand. Sophia saw the quick exchange of glances between Isaac and Mrs Gribbins and remembered how close they were to each other. She felt a strange pang of guilt that she had cut the woman out of Isaac's confinement.

'Girls, go to the dairy and bring some fresh cream and butter in. Not much, just a small jug and a half dish of butter. No need to rush back,' Mrs Gribbins ordered and the young kitchen hands quickly made themselves scarce.

Isaac looked up at Mrs Gribbins, whose hands had settled on her hips. 'Please do not say anything you might later regret, Mrs G,' Isaac said, resigned to the apparent fact that the woman intended to.

'You drink your wine and do not try to stand up for me just yet, lad,' Mrs Gribbins told him and then presented herself before Sophia. 'That man —' she pointed at Isaac who was shifting his weight in the chair as if he wished he could just vanish with the maids — 'is worth far more than that Mr Huntley fellow any day of the week. You, Miss Sophia, are right for him and he for you, but that other man is a waste of a —'

'Mrs G!' Isaac snapped and she glanced at him and nodded. 'I told you to have faith and patience. All will be well . . .'

'That other gentleman is no gentleman and I would not want to see you hitched to him, Miss Sophia. And I know it's none of my business, and I'm well aware that speaking like this could get me turned out, just like young Isaac here was back in the day.'

That comment hurt Sophia. It was meant to, for Sophia realised that in Mrs Gribbins' eyes the wrong had been Sophia's. 'Then why would you risk all to make such a bold claim, Mrs Gribbins? You know I care only for Isaac — you of all people have seen the proof of this. I do not understand why you should be so vocal now. I think you need to explain yourself,' Sophia said and softened her tone as she looked to Isaac who had clenched his hand into a fist, his face creased with concern.

'Oh, I shall, and you be quiet, Isaac, because this needs plain woman talk. Mr Huntley made a play for our Annie, the scullery maid, and that ain't right, nor fair either. Maisey had already managed to brush him off earlier in the week. But Annie is no more than fourteen summers! The girl ran into the woods to get away from him and it was all I could do to get her to come back inside the Hall again. He won't get no chance to finish off what he started; I can assure you of that! Even if we all get thrown out on the dung heap together! So I'm going to see your father and, if he turns me out, then shame on him and the lot of you!' Mrs Gribbins sniffed, her colour very high.

'Mrs G! Enough now,' Isaac insisted. 'You will not go to Sir Kenneth. I will tell him. He has a lot to think on today as it is. Please leave it to me,' he said.

'No, you won't, Isaac, for if you do the outcome could be dire for you,' Sophia said and looked at Mrs Gribbins. 'And for us. You have every reason to want to discredit him, whereas Mrs Gribbins and the scullery maid have much to lose. That can only go a long way to show that there is no reason why they would not tell Sir Kenneth the truth.'

Mrs Gribbins began to untie her apron.

'However, you will not speak with him either, Mrs Gribbins,' Sophia insisted. 'Not on your own. I shall.'

Isaac nodded. 'Mr Huntley has debts, Sophia. The message that was sent today is proof. I have already shown your father so he has been warned of Lucas Huntley's character. Do not repeat that though, either of you. If you do, I shall be discredited in Sir Kenneth's eyes and that we cannot afford.'

'If Mr Huntley has wronged this maid then he should make amends to her and answer for it,' Sophia said. 'But if it is her word against his . . . then . . . This girl, did he . . . I mean, is there any chance that she may be . . . ?' Sophia's resolve was fading fast.

'No, miss, he was interrupted before that happened, but he would have gone through with it and he has frightened her right good,' Mrs Gribbins explained.

'Very well. You will make sure the girl has rest and a drink of what Isaac is having.' Sophia stopped as Mrs Gribbins' shock was instantly apparent.

'That's the best wine.'

'This girl needs a fine cooked meal and a glass of wine. It will not erase the memory of her abuser, but it will provide good sustenance which will help her recover. I would also have her know that she has my promise that it will never happen again.' Sophia's words were emphatic.

Mrs Gribbins nodded her agreement. 'Very well. You always were a good lass, if a little headstrong. Just right for my Isaac,' she added.

'Isaac, I will see Father,' Sophia said.

'You stay safe here, or find Judd if you must, and I will find you later to tell you what is happening.' In her heart she felt all would work itself out somehow, but she must speak with her father. Lucas Huntley apparently felt he had the right to take whatever he wanted. Well he would not have her, or anyone else in her household. She would stop Mr Huntley's plans and have him sent on his way.

28

Isaac left Mrs Gribbins to sort out the distressed maid and start the preparations for dinner. How he was going to sit down at a table with Lucas Huntley if Sir Kenneth had not already rousted the cad from the estate, he did not know. But the ways of 'polite society' were strange to him. Debts could be ignored, obscene behaviour to a maid dismissed as 'a bit of fun', so he knew not to let his hopes rise too high. Yet he doubted that Sir Kenneth would now let Sophia go off with such a man.

He crossed over the cobblestones using his crutches with care, knowing that the two men were out riding and that he would be able to speak to Robert in private. He needed to see the place that his father died. He needed more information about his father's death. Something did not sit right.

'Robert,' he called out as he entered

the stables.

Silence.

Looking around the stalls and seeing the ladder at the end of the building, he swallowed. Those steps led to the private space that had been where he and his father lived for years, and the memories were overwhelming, or rather the emotions that they triggered were. He took a moment and walked to the back of the empty stall and leaned against the wall. He did not wish to risk climbing the ladder. Besides, it represented the past and he was not ready to face that again just yet.

The place was not as well organised as it had been back in his father's day, yet this empty stall was clean and had fresh hay scattered over the floor. This seemed odd. The more he looked around the more this stall stood out. With the edge of one crutch, he pushed at the hay until he found what he sought, the hatch. In his father's day, it had not been used, but as he crouched down he could see that the metal loop that served as a handle had been replaced. He pushed the rest of the hay aside and the door could clearly be seen. Lifting the loop, he raised the door. Hooked on the underside was a lantern. He could see a ladder leading down to the empty space below. It too had been replaced.

Curiosity got the better of him. He looked around for the tinderbox which he knew would be clipped near the lamp. He lit it and set it aside then carefully lay down on the floor of the stall and lowered the lamp, looking in awe at what he saw. Far from being empty, the hold was stacked with goods. These were not the supplies of a stable; they were a stash of contraband. He could clearly see casks of brandy as well as what could be bricks of tobacco.

'What the hell are you doing, Robert?' he muttered, before putting out the lamp and shutting the trapdoor. He got to his feet, brushed himself down and pushed the hay evenly around the stall, just as it had been when he came in. He then clenched his lips together, for now he had yet another surprise to tell Sir Kenneth. Good God!

He was about to step out when Robert appeared at the corner of the stables.

'Isaac! You are a sight for sore eyes.' Robert smiled. 'You shouldn't be risking slipping on them stones though. If you want me, send Brent — he'd love that.'

Isaac did not move. 'I was looking for you.' Isaac watched his friend, the man he considered as a brother, but was seeing more the stranger that Sophia had described to him.

'I was in town. I've brought a letter back for Mr Huntley from his father. It was delivered yesterday apparently. Come and break bread with me,' Robert said and gestured towards the kitchen.

'No, not now. I want to know where my father fell, Robert. I want to know why he fell. I need to know the truth.' Isaac watched Robert's face contort. He was indeed hiding something beneath his pain; his smile had faded completely.

'Very well,' Robert said and walked past him into the stables. 'Why could you not just take my word for it?' Robert asked as he stopped by the empty stall. 'You had to dig deeper!'

'Because the truth has a way of working its way out of the darkness and into the light,' Isaac said.

Robert pointed to the passageway between the empty stall and the second one where a hunter was happily munching his fill.

'I found him lying there. He must have blacked out and hit his head on the rake as he fell. I doubt he knew much about it . . .' Robert swallowed. 'If I could have been here, if I could have helped him, don't you think that I would have?' Robert breathed deeply and shook his head. 'You do not understand, you couldn't, you were out being a hero!' His words were snapped out like poison darts. 'He should have come with me to the inn. He was supposed to come with me, but he did not arrive. A horse had been in foal. All had gone well but he wanted to stay a while and follow on later, but he didn't, did he? He stayed with the blasted horse!

He should never have even been in the stable,' Robert said and wiped his eyes with the back of his hand.

'My God, Robert, was he murdered?' Isaac took a step towards Robert and shoved him against the wall. 'You knew this and did nothing? You covered for the killer? Who did it?' Isaac watched Robert's face crumble like a child's.

'I loved him too, but I wasn't his son, always in your shadow, never good enough . . .'

'Why? You had a home, you had his love, he trained you . . . You had him when I was sent away and still that was not enough.'

'You even had the heart of Miss Sophia; she never even met my eyes.'

Understanding dawned in Isaac's mind. 'You told me that day that Sir Kenneth would not arrive back till dinner, but you knew he would arrive earlier, didn't you? It's your fault I got sent away!' Isaac saw him colour and knew the truth.

'Yes, I knew, but then why should you

get away with it. The two of you. You never knew your place. Not then, not now!'

'Robert, give me Mr Huntley's letter.' Isaac snatched it and put it in his pocket. 'Now leave here and go far away. You have tonight to do so. Tomorrow I will tell what I know to Sir Kenneth and he can decide what should be done.' Isaac walked to the doorway.

'I loved him,' Robert said.

'So did I!' Isaac said, and returned to the Hall.

29

Sir Kenneth ordered Sophia to find Lucas Huntley and bring him to his study.

Sophia found him and passed the message on.

'Thank you,' he said, and stormed straight past her.

Isaac gestured ever so slightly with his eyes that Sophia should follow him.

Sophia followed Lucas Huntley back into the study, slipping inside, and closed the door behind her.

Sir Kenneth held out a letter that Lucas immediately ripped open. Lucas had his back to her and so was unaware of her presence.

He balled a fist and let out a loud sigh. 'It appears, sir, I have a new problem. My father has taken ill. His heart apparently is tired and needs rest. So I must return before the day is out.' He sighed and scrunched up the letter into a ball, his knuckles white.

'I am sorry to learn of this, Lucas. Do they have any notion as to how long it will be before he recovers?' Sir Kenneth asked.

'They do not know.' Lucas waved his arms upwards and let them fall as if devoid of hope. It was indeed a theatrical gesture, Sophia thought, ungraciously. 'And I am to return without a settlement being agreed. Will you approve the proposal I seek so that I can go to him and fill his tired heart with joy?' Lucas stood square before her father. 'If all our plans fall apart now he may be undone and I would leave these shores knowing he may never join me.'

'I will do better than that, my dear Lucas.' Sir Kenneth slapped him on the back and seemed instantly full of good cheer, which shocked Sophia.

Sophia's heart raced. Whatever was he about to say? Should she blurt out about Lucas's poor conduct, here, now?

Sir Kenneth placed his hands on the younger man's shoulders. 'I will ride back with you. We shall deliver our good news together!'

Lucas paled and visibly stumbled over his hesitant words in response. 'Sir, that is generous, but there is no need for you to exert yourself. You are needed here, Sir Kenneth! I shall return alone, as I must.'

'Nonsense, man! I know when I am needed elsewhere. It is obvious that my duty is to be at the side of my wife's old friend. Sophia and my estate manager will do an admirable job here in my absence, won't you, Sophia?' her father said and Lucas's head shot around.

She was not sure what Lucas's look conveyed, but she did not care for it. Was it anger that she should be privy to men's conversation?

'Yes, Father,' she replied.

'Good. Go and tell Cynthia I will be returning with Lucas Huntley.'

* * *

Sophia burst into the study as she returned, having not found Cynthia, but her father was not there. Instead, Cynthia was standing by the fireside with an unfolded letter in her hand. For a moment Sophia thought it must be Isaac's reply from London, but then she realised that it had been scrunched up. It must have been the one Lucas had discarded.

'What does it say?' Sophia asked, and stood listening in disbelief as the words were read out.

'Lucas. Why have you not sent word? Do not fail me again! If you must leave the blasted sheep at least get the filly. Tell them I am weakening and need this match to give me hope. I await good news. If Sir K is hesitant make sure that you compromise his whelp. Seduce her, damn you, and have this deal sealed. Time is running out for us.'

'Has Father left?' Sophia swallowed.

'No, not yet. You see, whilst you were chasing around, I came in here, found this and shared it with him. He is currently preparing to leave with Lucas Huntley, but he has more to say to his father than the man is expecting.' Cynthia cocked her head to one side with a self-satisfied smile spreading across her face.

'There is something else Father should know, Cynthia. Mr Huntley assaulted a young maid called Annie.'

'He may have, but that will not cut much sway with him, as some see it, as simply a perk of owning a house like this. Men abuse their positions and she would not be the first woman to succumb to the flattery of a handsome man with a honeyed tongue.'

'That is preposterous! How can a scullery maid defend herself against a wealthy man? Father would never . . .' Sophia looked at Cynthia's calm expression.

'My dear, Mrs Gribbins was young once,' Cynthia explained.

'No!' Sophia could not take this latest revelation in. 'Never, Father would never have . . .'

'Oh, yes, and he regrets it dearly because she lost the child he gave her, and then she could have no more, which is why Isaac is so special to her. He found a child who needed a mother whose father worked on the estate, and so they were moved close and the lad worked in the stables and was nurtured by Mrs Gribbins.' Cynthia shrugged. 'He did what he could to make amends.'

'How would you know this when you were not even here, Cynthia?' Sophia could hardly believe what Cynthia implied.

'Because he told me, Sophia. You see, Kenneth and I do not have many secrets between us, unlike you and your father.'

Sophia bridled and left the room, filled with emotions that felt as though they would make her heart and her head burst if she did not find her father before he left.

* * *

Isaac stood in front of Robert. 'I told you to leave!' he said. 'Well you have blown your chances.'

'We've worked the night. The goods

are all gone. I've wiped the slate, Isaac. They won't come here again. The man who hit Joshua never meant to kill him. Your pa hit his head as he fell. That said, they have a way of meting out justice to their own. Joshua was well liked hereabouts. The man was sent to apologise to him personally like.'

'And you expect my forgiveness?' Isaac said.

'No, never. Nor do I want it for it is your father's I want and God's. I spoke to Sir Kenneth. I will be leaving. But I will have somewhere to go.'

'Where's that?' Isaac asked, wondering what tale he had spun to Sir Kenneth, but he did not doubt for one moment that the goods had been taken away.

'Australia,' he said. 'I asked Mr Huntley if he could do with a good landsman who knew all about horses. When he leaves, I do too,' Robert said and sniffed.

'Well you were going there in chains, so perhaps it is better that you go there as a free man.'

Isaac walked away.

* * *

Sophia ran upstairs to her father's bedchamber, but he was not there. She was about to return, hoping that if he were in the stables she would be able to keep him there for a few moments. The thought of him having been intimate with Mrs Gribbins made her stomach turn over.

It was only when a hand grabbed her arm and swung her around that she was aware that Lucas was still upstairs. He had dropped his bag by the door as he was leaving. He pulled her back into the shadows, covering her mouth with his and pushing her hard against the wall.

Her breath was rapid as he released her, but she could not pull away from his weight. He held her hands down at her sides and quickly slipped them behind her back, leaning into her.

'I will scream,' she said, panic building.

'Go on, for then you and I will be compromised. Our tryst laid bare.'

Repulsed, she headbutted the bridge

of his nose.

He yelped as he staggered backwards holding his face. It had not been hard enough to break his nose but certainly stunned him. 'You bitch!' he said, but she was out of the door, down the stairs and into her father's arms before he reached the top of them.

'What happened?' Sir Kenneth asked.

Cynthia looked on from the study doorway.

'Mr Huntley tried to fulfil his father's orders,' she explained, then stood back from her father and stared up at him. 'The man is a cad. He tried to rape one of our maids,' she said, then glanced at Cynthia.

'No, I did not,' Lucas interrupted. 'The girl tried to improve her station in life and begged me to take her away with me, but I told her to be on her way. Should we go, sir?' he asked Sir Kenneth.

'No, we shall not! You treat my daughter abysmally, you have your debtors on your heels,' Sir Kenneth said, 'and you expect me to seriously offer you her hand in marriage?' He shook his head. 'You are beneath contempt. I now own your debts. I own you!'

'I don't think so. We have been discussing strategies, have we not, Isaac?' Lucas looked to the corridor where Isaac was reappearing slowly leaning on his crutch.

'Indeed, we have,' Isaac admitted. 'You see, for Lucas's daring plan to work he needed a respectable witness who could whisper in the right ears that I had seen Sophia willingly enjoying the close affections of Mr Lucas Huntley. If such a rumour were to reach the circuit of the gentleman's clubs then Mr Huntley had deduced that no one would marry her, save for a lowly lieutenant who had risen in the ranks. Something you would never wish upon your only offspring. So, to avert this shameful downfall, the answer that Lucas Huntley has come up with is simple: you let him wed Sophia and the stain and disgrace is taken away to Australia with them. He would pay me a sum of fifteen guineas to play along,' Isaac said, as Lucas's self-satisfied expression grew into a grin.

'So, Sir Kenneth, your Sophia will be mine or will be disgraced — the choice is yours.'

Sir Kenneth glared at Isaac. 'You would go along with this after everything I have done for you?' His fists were balled, but Sophia did not doubt that it was Isaac who played a cunning game here.

'Yes, I played along, but you have no need to abide this scoundrel any longer in your house, for he is beneath the lowest creature I have ever seen in any conflict. I would never betray Sophia, or yourself, sir,' Isaac declared.

'You bloody fool!' Lucas yelled at Isaac. 'Was it more money you wanted? Was that it?'

'No.' Lucas made to come at him, but Isaac held a pistol that he slipped out from underneath his jacket. 'You see, I have no need of your money for I have been busy making my own these last five years. Whilst you whored, I fought and earned my reward.'

'You are from the dung heap and will

forever be so. Money will not buy you the rank and education of a gentleman,' Lucas declared.

'If you shoot him now we will all give witness he attacked you,' Cynthia said.

Sophia gasped as she was not at all certain Cynthia's words were meant as a bluff.

Lucas stood back. He grabbed his coat and bag and backed out of the front door where his horse was already saddled. Robert Judd held the reins of the man's horse and had a pack tied to the back of his own.

Sir Kenneth said, 'You will leave and tell your father he will hear from my solicitor before the end of the month.'

Lucas left at speed.

Isaac placed the gun back in his pocket. He looked up at Sir Kenneth. 'It isn't even loaded. I thought to have it with me in case Lucas Huntley and I came to blows. I am disadvantaged at the moment,' he said coyly.

'We need a port or a sherry. Come into my study.'

Sophia poured out three glasses of port. Sir Kenneth looked at her in surprise as she handed a glass to each of them and sipped her own.

'What a mess this is. He may say what he likes and our name will be tainted.' Sir Kenneth shook his head.

'That he won't,' Isaac said confidently. 'You own his debt, remember. You can have them ruined before they set sail. I wanted to gift you this debt for your leverage as a thank you for the kindness you have showed me and Mrs Gribbins over the years,' he added, and Sophia saw her father's cheeks colour at the mention of their cook. She knew instantly that Cynthia's words were true. 'And for the care of my father's last arrangements. If needs be I can buy myself a higher commission and return to prove myself more worthy of Sophia.'

'Isaac, no! You nearly died once already. Father, you cannot let him do this. He has done everything to be a good friend to me and to this family. Is it not enough that he has earned position, wealth and has been injured? Would you send him back again?' Sophia pleaded.

'I need time,' Sir Kenneth replied. 'We all need time. This has gone very badly. Lucas Huntley will pay for the abuse he has put upon my household. The money will be repaid with interest. Isaac I thank you for you acted quickly, but heed my words, never presume to act in my name again without my full knowledge or you will not be able to stand again in this lifetime. Do I make myself clear?'

'Yes, sir,' Isaac said as any good soldier would to his commanding officer.

'Now leave, the pair of you, and the same terms of your stay are to be adhered to. Break them and I will not even consider your union.'

'Yes, sir,' they both chirped up.

Isaac left. Before Sophia followed, she looked back at her father.

'Mrs Gribbins?' she asked.

'Do not risk a conversation into areas that do not concern you. Do I make myself clear?'

'Yes, sir,' she said.

Epilogue

'Isaac! How marvellous!' Cynthia cried. Everyone stood and clapped as Isaac entered the morning room without his stick. 'Only one month and you are healed, and how much has happened in that short time.'

Isaac limped into the Hall, standing tall and proud, and with almost a straight gait. It felt so good. This was a moment in his life he would never forget. How lucky he was to have kept the leg at all, but to be able to walk again unaided was all down to the care he had received here.

Sophia was so happy to see him, but there was sadness in his heart. For what excuse now was there for him to stay longer? He had mended — well, not enough to ride and return to his duties — but enough to stand without support.

Sir Kenneth stood up. 'You are walking straight and proud. Good man!' he said and came to greet him with a hug.

‘It is all thanks to your generosity and kindness, sir.’ Isaac knew he could never repay such a debt. ‘We need to talk, sir,’ Isaac said.

‘Sit and talk with my dear Cynthia. I have something that I have to do.’ Sir Kenneth looked away and Isaac felt rejected after building his hopes up for this moment. As if sensing he had been rather abrupt, Sir Kenneth added, ‘We’ll talk, but later. The women have much to say, as always.’

* * *

Staring at the rhubarb in the cottage garden at the back of the Hall, Sir Kenneth was in deep thought.

‘Give you a penny for them,’ Mrs Gribbins said and stood alongside him. ‘You have the look of a troubled man, sir.’

‘You haven’t got a penny to give, wench,’ he said and heard her chuckle in return. It was a good hearty honest laugh.

'That's where you are wrong because young Isaac has seen me right,' she said.

Sir Kenneth looked at her. 'Then why are you still here? You could be free of me, of the estate, of your chores.' He shook his head and looked at her. 'He has a generous spirit; I'll give you that.'

She turned to face him. 'This is your home and ours too. You are our master and we love you because you treat us all right. We share your wealth because you allow us to live well here. None of us want to leave. We want for nothing. Where would we go? And young Isaac is a lovely man. Sophia could do no better . . .'

'You know I cannot say yes to him. He has no heritage . . .' Sir Kenneth's voice almost broke with emotion.

'No, and neither had I. Our love was thrashed, but did it ever really go away?' She tilted her head on one side and he had to look away.

'I loved my wife . . .' he began.

'Aye, I loved her too, for it was not of her doing she was matched like a prize cow to a bull.'

'You are crude, woman,' he snapped, but did not walk away.

'Aye, and you laughed at that once and fell in love with my honesty when all around you sat on circumstance. I beg you, Kenneth, do not let two hearts break again. He has money, he has honour and he wants to stay here,' she began, but Sir Kenneth spun around to face her.

'From where? He must have stolen it. I cannot accept that.'

'Yes you can, for he did you a great service with Mr Huntley and do not think so badly of him. He found it buried, like treasure.'

Cynthia appeared and Sir Kenneth moved away from Mrs Gribbins.

Cynthia smiled. 'Kenneth, let those two young people who are so much in love live their lives together with your blessing. It matters not from where he came because he has risen high and he could be the breath of fresh air this place needs.'

'She is my heir, Cynthia. Tradition

dictates . . .' Sir Kenneth began, but his words drifted off into nothingness.

'Yes, I know, but she may not be for much longer, for you will have another child by Christmas.' Cynthia's eyes sparkled as realisation dawned in Sir Kenneth's face. 'So let them be engaged to each other and declare it proudly to the world. But, Mrs Gribbins, keep this news to yourself for I will only announce it when they have their future sorted.'

'I'll make a special celebration cake, miss.'

Cynthia and Sir Kenneth laughed as Mrs Gribbins ran back to her kitchen.

Sophia and Isaac entered the garden to find out what Mrs Gribbins' squeals of delight were about. Sir Kenneth tried to compose himself as wave after wave of good news seem to put at rest years of guilty secrets.

'Whatever is wrong, Father?' Sophia asked.

'Nothing, nothing. I am to give a father's blessing to you both and we will be one happy family again after you two are wed!' he said proudly and swept them into a big hug.

Cynthia looked on and shook her head. 'Men can't keep a secret to save their lives,' she whispered and winked at Sophia's delighted face, as she held tightly to Isaac who had all but crumpled too.

A Note to the Reader

Dear Reader,

Thank you for choosing to read *In Sickness and In Health*.

The Early Nineteenth Century

The early nineteenth century was a period of great conflict and change: a time of war, pressgangs, and extreme social, agricultural, religious and political changes. All these impacted on the ordinary people who were left behind, whilst the wars with Napoleon dragged on.

The countryside was changing as mills were being built and cottage industries suffered, along with their communities. The population gravitated to these places of work and life in the countryside changed.

The government taxed its people harshly, whilst still fearing the possibility of a revolution as had happened in France. It was hardly surprising then that smuggling and opportunists abounded, yet in plying the trade they gave coin to an enemy. Some gangs were known for their violence, others were less so and merely supplied a ready market that crossed over social rank and was often funded by a moneyed man.

With the onset of the Industrial Revolution, Luddite activities and the growth of new money, lives were changing and the old money was feeling threatened.

In the cities 'society' had strict rules: influence and connections were so very important.

In my books the settings are more remote. These influences mean nothing when a character is dealing with survival, either their own or someone who they have met. So boundaries are crossed, rules of society are broken or are made irrelevant.

The Region

Most of my titles are set in an area of the country that I love: North Yorkshire, with its beautiful coast and moors.

My villages of Beckton and Gorebeck are based upon typical North Yorkshire market towns, such as: Guisborough, Yarm, Thirsk, Helmsley. By 1815 both have their own small mills situated just outside the towns.

Ebton is based on the well-known Victorian town of Saltburn-by-the-Sea, North Yorkshire, only my version is as I imagine it to have been at the turn of the nineteenth century.

The essence of The Yorkshire Saga series

Love is a timeless essential of life. Throughout history, love in all its forms is a constant: be it passionate, caring, needy, manipulative, possessive or one that is strong enough to cross barriers of culture or faith. When two souls meet in a situation which takes them out of their normal social strata or into a shared danger, a relationship forms as the adventure unfolds.

If you enjoyed reading *In Sickness and In Health* I would really appreciate it if you could take a moment to leave a review either on Amazon or Goodreads, or wherever you wish.

It is always helpful to read feedback and I am always interested in what my readers think, or would like to read next.

I can be contacted on:

Facebook: ValerieHolmesAuthor

Twitter: @ValerieHolmesUK

Or through my website:

www.ValerieHolmesAuthor.com

Love the Adventure!

Valerie Holmes